PURSUED
A BILLIONAIRE'S OBSESSION

A Complete Novel By
CHRISTINE GRAY

PURSUED

Remember....

You haven't read 'til you've read #Royalty

Check us out at
www.royaltypublishinghouse.com
Royalty drops #dopebooks

PURSUED

OTHER TITLES BY *CHRISTINE GRAY*
THE BILLONAIRE MOB WIFE

OTHER TITLE UNDER THE PEN NAME *SAPPHIRE*:
DON'T TELL MY HUSBAND SERIES
FALLING FOR AN ALPHA BILLIONAIRE SERIES
CONSUMED BY LOVE
AN EXTRAORDINARY LOVE SERIES
ONE OF A KIND LOVE SERIES

Dear Readers,

I'm back again for another drama, laughter, and sexy filled ride. This is only the FIRST of complete novels involving this family. Also, keep a look out for hints of other stories that I have cooking up to be released later this year. As always, I hope that message from this book shines through in the mist of all the alpha, and sexy that I love to create.

Till Then, Enjoy!!!

PURSUED

Chapter One

Pike tapped his finger on the polished dark wood table top. His emerald green eyes sparkled with laughter as he listened to his parents. Their words were more comical than anything else. He had heard this speech so much over the last year, that now he just sat back and enjoyed it. Although their words were mostly directed to his younger brother, he knew that he was also included in the sermon that featured a lot of shouting and empty threats. He fought to keep a straight face when his mother joined in. She had this way of talking with her hands that always captivated him. It was her facial expressions with her eyes growing in size when she wanted to stress a point that made him want to laugh. He intently, locked his gaze on his brother's plate to keep from losing.

"This shit isn't going to fly any longer, boys. I mean it. If you don't get serious, then I...I," Flustered, Olivia's words trailed off.

"You'll what, Mother? Lock us in our rooms? Or better yet, I haven't been over a lady's knee in a minute," winked Brick.

"Not in front of the child," she warned. Her eyes cut to the little boy sitting next to her son.

The cute boy looked up into his father's face and frowned. "I don't know why you would want to get on a lady's lap. That shit always hurts when Nana spanks me."

Unable to hold it back, Pike burst out into a fit of laughter, followed by both his brother and father. The fact that his mother was glaring at them, with her extra-large eyes, only made matters worse.

"This is exactly what I'm talking about. Your boy is only four, and he's already talking like some gutter rat," she pointed out.

Brick winked at his little boy, leaned over, and whispered in his ear. The boy nodded.

"I'm sorry, Nana. I'll choose my words better next time," promised the boy.

PURSUED

The handsome, older man sitting to her right placed his hand on hers to tell her to hold it. Even though he was in his sixties, weathered by years of hard work, he still had no issues with women throwing themselves at him. His tall, muscular built had been passed on to his sons he noticed. He knew that they were handsome. Unlike him at their age, all he had was a strong back and his looks, and that was all he needed to get under skirts in his day. Now his son's also had a vast fortune to add to that combination that helped to gain them entry into any pussy they set their sights on. He stroked his ginger goatee before he spoke.

"I don't like you all making fun of your mother. You know she only means the best for you. I know how it is boys, believe me. But this shit has to stop. I think we have turned a blind eye long enough," he paused as he trained his eyes on Brick. "I'm sick of cleaning up your messes, and although, Pike hasn't been as transparent with his activities, you're no better. I've raised you, both to be men, but everything you have and stand to gain is from me. I hate to play this hand, but if you two fuck up again, there won't be a choice in the matter," explained Forrester, slowly to ensure that his message was understood.

Out of respect, Pike and Brick nodded, but they both knew that there was only so much their father could do to them at their age. Not only that, but Pike had made his first million when he was twenty over; thirteen years ago, and Brick when he was twenty-two over nine years ago. They had created their own divisions of their father's company that they operated solely. Their father meant every word, but they were spoken more so for the sake of their mother. Even though that was a fact, neither one wanted to cross the man. He was a cunning son-of-a-bitch that seemed to always get his way, no matter the cost.

"I can assume by your clothes that you won't be staying the night?" sighed Forrester. He already knew what they were up to. He had heard the car service at the front door a few hours ago. If that wasn't a giveaway, the tailored suit, and tie attire, his boys were both deck out in was a dead giveaway. At times, he cursed the day that he had taken them along with him, years ago for a night out. He had thought that it would have been a good outlet for their carnal desires without any consequences. He had been half right. After Brick's baby, he had chosen his lovers better. Pike, on the other hand, seemed only to go to Ginger Island for the company of a woman. He appeared to have no desire at all for the women in their circles that were breaking their necks to bed him in hopes of capturing his heart. According to his spies, he wasn't taken with any one women on the island, but it still bothered him.

"Yes, we're flying out for the evening," answered Pike, checking his watch.

Forrester held up his hand to stop Olivia from complaining.

"You can't expect them to be monks. They have needs, and what better place than there for them to get it. Enjoy yourselves, sons," he chuckled.

"Can you tuck me in?" The little boy asked, hopefully.

"And Uncle Pike will tell the story," offered Brick, which made his son dance on his feet.

"Really?! I like the noises and voices he makes better than yours, daddy."

"If I had a dime for every time I've heard how much better I am than your Daddy, I would be rich," winked Pike.

Three hours later, Pike and Brick sat in the tan leather seats of the small airplane as they sipped the amber-colored whiskey. Brick glanced out the window over the midnight water.

"I'm sorry."

Pike's ginger colored eyebrow shot up as he regarded his younger brother.

"For?" he asked as if he didn't know.

"They won't be coming down on us so hard if-"

"Bullshit. You did nothing wrong, and you know it. I'm actually happy that I have a little nephew to corrupt," he smiled as he kicked his brother in his shin.

"I know, but we all can't be like you," teased Brick.

"Actually, you can. They can't get knocked up if they swallow."

Pike laughed at Brick's shocked expression. Followed by a look of disgust.

"Shit, I don't mind a good bj as a teaser, but there's nothing like burying my cock in that hot, wet pussy. If that's all you get from here, then why the fuck are you going twice a month?" questioned Brick before he went still. He narrowed his eyes as he pinned Pike with his green gaze. He began to shake his head slowly. Pike glanced out the window, but not before his brother read the truth in his eyes.

"You know that will never work, Pike. You need to leave that alone," he warned.

"Yeah, I know, and I will...soon," mumbled Pike.

All eyes were on the striking pair as they entered the massive mansion. Both men were tall, broad, and muscular. Pike had brushed his ginger and brown hair back into a ponytail. His hair curled at the ends to rest on the collar of his white shirt. It didn't matter that the place was filled to the gills with men all there for the same reason; female companionship of the finest quality. The most exclusive brothel in the world only catered to the richest clients around the globe. Three hundred sixty-five days a year, in different locations, it offered the men and women that were fortunate enough to gain entry a variety of ladies from all around the world, in all shapes, sizes, and talents. One by one, the women all stole looks at the brothers as they mingled through the reception room off of the double French doors that, were used as a front door from the fragrant garden that let the cool tropical breeze in.

"Shouldn't you be focusing on that old man?" grumbled Elysia, grabbing the girl by the shoulder. She had seen Pike and Brick enter the house, too.

Fara smiled. "You don't have to worry. I'll take care of him after I talk to Pike."

"Some of us would like to try him out, you know."

"He comes here for me."

"I don't think so, Boo. We all know what he's here for," frowned Elysia. She couldn't stand the uppity bitch. If Fara wasn't going to step aside to let her play with the handsome man, then she was going to put the chick in her place. "I bet he closes his eyes while he's fucking your mouth so he can imagine he's with her," she added in a whisper as she pointed into the crowd.

Fara heard her laughter as she followed the woman's direction to see Pike pause, long enough to talk to his brother, before he made a beeline to the woman that was surrounded by a group of men in the corner.

***

It was strange how she was able to sense him before she actually saw him strolling through the open doors. The leisurely way he moved made him look more like a lion than a man. His confidence was both alluring and unnerving at the same time. Her eyes scanned his body while he stood some distance away as he spoke with his brother. Pike had brushed his ginger and brown hair back into a ponytail. His hair curled at the ends to rest on the collar of his white shirt. Even dressed in a nicely made suit for the office, he and his brother stood out above the rest. Her eyes only strayed for a moment to his brother, Brick. The younger brother was handsome and cheerful as always, but she knew that the majority of her evening was going to be spent with Pike. She knew why he had come there. His visits had become predictable now, and for those rare occasions, that business kept him from showing up, he always sent her a text even though he didn't own her any explanations.

She sighed under her breath before she responded to one of the gentlemen that were hoping to bed her that night. They all came with the intention of being the one to get in between her thighs; only to give up as the night drug on. It was a known fact that Cashmere didn't fuck anyone. She ran the brothel. She was the Head Mistress, which meant that she didn't have to spread it wide and thin like the other women in the house. She shifted in her chair as the dull throbbing; she always experienced when Pike's visits, started to build. She knew that her thoughts were going to be filled with the image of that man for days long after he left.

Why don't you just fuck him? The nagging voice in her head begged.

She shook her head as if the voice was one of the men that were crowded around her. She had never taken Pike to her bed, and she damn sure wasn't going to do so now. No, the time that they spent together was purely a friendly one. They would talk, walk through the garden, play video games, or chess, or just watch TV. Although she knew that he wouldn't mind taking their friendship to a sexual relationship, Cashmere wasn't stupid. They had shared too much as friends for anything physical between them not to eventually snowball into deeper feelings or love.

She frowned when she caught herself straightening her hair as he approached her. Frustrated, she intently replaced the thick locks back over her forehead. It was a good thing that this would be their last visit for a while. She was sure that after she returned from her vacation; all nice and round with a baby in her stomach, there would be no issues with keeping their relationship just a friendship. The mood of the gathered men around her seemed to change when they caught a glimpse of Pike heading their way. The ones that knew him were already mumbling under their breath and whispering to the other men. They knew that with Pike being there that meant that Cashmere would be leaving to be with the handsome man. She could hear the envy in the men's voices as they excused themselves to pair off with one of the girls, or to get a drink, or head to the casino.

"Hello Gorgeous," smiled Pike as he feasted upon her. Her beauty and effortless sexiness always took him off guard. She didn't have to dress in short, tight, or revealing clothing to get attention. Eyes just naturally gravitated to her. The combination of her thick hair; that was now twisted to resemble dreads to fall past her shoulder blades, her mocha colored smooth skin, full lips, large almond shaped light brown eyes, and fit, shapely body was a lethal mixture for any man.

He leaned down and planted a whispery kiss on her cheek. The fact that she was short was a turn on for him. He wanted to dominate her under his large, muscular body. They both lingered as they breathed in the other's scent. Cashmere smelled like *Lander's oatmeal* soap; he knew she preferred while he smelled of a maleness and expensive cologne. He finally took a step back to gaze down into her face. It bothered him that she wouldn't make eye contact with him.

"I brought us something new for tonight. I had to pull some strings, but..." he let his words trail off as he reached into his coat pocket. He had been waiting for days to see her expression. He had no doubt that what he had would get her out of whatever funk she was in. He could tell that she was having a problem making out what was so important about the disk he had produced as he waved it before her face.

Her entire face lit up as she read the words that had been written in black sharpie. She practically took his fingers off. She snatched the disk just that fast.

"Are you joking?" she asked, breathlessly. At the slow shake of his head, she let out a loud scream as she threw herself into his arms.

He gladly held her to his chest. Pike clenched his teeth as the urge to draw her closer to his body so she could feel his stiff dick. His hands itched to fall to her round ass. By the time, she broke away; his heated thoughts were hidden behind his emerald green eyes.

"How the hell did you manage to get a copy of the new *JK Rowling* movie before it came to the theaters? You know what? I don't care," she tossed over her shoulder. She had already started towards the stairs. Pike had to lengthen his strides to keep up with her.

"I thought a closet nerd like you would appreciate the offering," he chuckled.

"Damn right," she admitted.

Pike slipped out of his coat and tossed it on the couch after he shut the door to her private apartment on the third floor. In spite of the fact that he had been in the private quarters many times, he always felt excited. Her place was inviting and comfortable with a gray comfortable couch set, eye-popping coral colored walls with white wainscot throughout, plush light gray carpet, and a large fireplace that dominated the room with an equally large flat screen mounted above it. He listened to her babble on as she busied herself trying to locate the remotes to get their viewing started. He took his time pouring himself a glass of *Hennessy*.

"How much?" he inquired as he held the bottle suspended over an empty glass.

"No... nothing for me," she stuttered.

He narrowed his eyes as he regarded her, silently. She looked beautiful as always in her cream colored muslin peasant dress that hung off of one of her shoulders. However, he couldn't shake the feeling that something was off with her.

"You know you can sip that over here," she smirked.

Pike chuckled at the way she plopped down on the sofa, tucking her feet under her bottom like a little girl.

She waited while he slowly crossed the room to her. She knew that in a few seconds he would sit next to her, place his drink on the table, then proceed to roll his shirt sleeves up. Her gaze followed the movement of his strong hands. Inch by inch the dark brown and ginger hair on his firm tanned forearms were revealed to her lustful eyes. Without words, she pushed the red button on the remote she held in her sweaty hands. She was sure that he could hear the loud gulp her throat made when she swallowed in an attempt to quench her dry throat.

"Are you alright?" He questioned.

She wanted to close her eyes and enjoy the feel of his warm hand on her shoulder. Instead, she jumped to her feet. She needed space. Quickly, she walked over to the switch on the wall and dimmed the lights. She cursed herself after she did it. He made a tasty vision on her couch.

"Yeah, everything is fine," she stated.

This time, when she sat down, she casually placed a pillow between them. Her act didn't go unnoticed. He chose to let it go, but a few minutes into the movie, he knocked the boundary to the ground. He saw her stiffen, but he didn't give a damn. He closed the gap between them before he settled back to watch the movie. Pike had never forced himself on her. He had never tried to cross the line she had clearly drawn in the sand. However, he wasn't going to be pushed away either.

Luckily, as the movie went on, Cashmere had loosened up. No longer was she stiff and aloft, but she began to laugh, touch him, and talk back to the screen which always made him laugh. After the hour and forty-five-minute screening ended; they continued to discuss the movie. Unfortunately, it didn't last. He saw a flicker in the depths of her brown eyes. It was as if she had just realized something she had forgotten. Once again, she was back to her strange way.

"What the hell is wrong with you?" he grunted.

"I was just thinking that Fara should be ready for you now."

He titled his head. "She lives here, Cashmere. It isn't as if she going to clock out and go home."

"Yes, I know, but it's getting late," she stated. She made a big show of glancing at the large grandfather clock that kept the time in the corner of the room.

"Does the brothel have new hours of operation?" he hissed.

She could tell he was getting annoyed. She had no choice but to tell him about her absence. She just hoped that he didn't press her to tell him more than what she was willing.

"I just have a million things to do before I leave in the morning."

Pike's eyebrow shot up in surprise. "Where are you going?" he asked, a bit too forcefully.

"I'm taking a much-needed vacation. Yep, an entire month of rest and relaxation," she beamed happily. She could almost see the hamster working on its wheel in his head as he tried to see if there was more to what she was saying.

He pinned her with his narrow gaze. She hadn't been with any of the men that visited the brothel in a very long time. Had that changed, he wondered. Was she really going to spend her time with another man away from the prying eyes of the staff?

"A vacation is good," he started slowly. "Is your mother tagging along?"

"No. She has to run the place while I'm away," she replied, getting to her feet. The fact that he remained seated made the butterflies in her stomach churn, nervously.

"Will you be vacationing alone?"

"Why would you ask such a crazy thing? Who the hell would be going with? Of course, I'm going by myself. Just me on the beaches of Miami," she answered, hotly. She prayed to God that she was convincing. She almost let out a loud sigh of relief at the dazzling smile he gave her.

"Why not travel a little further? You can stay at one of my places in New York. I can move things around on my calendar to take you around and show you a good time. Besides, South Florida is just like Ginger Island," he pointed out.

Cashmere tilted her head as she stared off into the distance. She was clever enough not to refuse his offer outright. Instead, she put on a show of actually considering his offer before she shot it down.

"No, I want it just to be me. Although your offer and company is great, I'm always with people. I need time for me," she smiled.

"Then have fun," he chuckled. He got to his feet to tower over her. "Let's have a quick smoke before I leave. I'm going to miss you when you're gone," he confessed as he walked toward his jacket to retrieve the tightly rolled joint. He leaned over, reached out his hand for his jacket, then went deathly still at her response.

"No! I'm really tired, and if I smoke out with you, I'll get none of this packing done."

Pike glared down at his jacket for a split second. This had been the fourth time she had not smoked with him. Nor had she drunken nothing more than water or juice when she had been with him. By the time, he straightened up and turned back around to face her; his doubts were hidden behind a mask.

"That's fine. I think I'll hit the casino before I go to Fara's room," he laughed while he slipped back on his suit jacket.

Cashmere tilted her head as he left the room. Quickly, she ran to the door and locked it. There was something strange in the way he looked before he left. She had never seen that expression on his handsome, chiseled face before. It sent a chill down her spine. The crooked smile on his lips seemed genuine, but the coldness in his eyes was frightening.

Pike heard the thud of the lock on the other side of the door.

Vacation my ass, he fumed as he began to walk down the hall toward the stairs. She was up to something. He was startled out of his thoughts at the sound of the loud voices surrounding him. He hadn't noticed that he had walked back down the stairs and into the casino. He remained still for a few more seconds as he scanned the smoky room. His eyes widened over the high pitch whistle that came from across the room. Quickly, he marched over and took a seat next to Brick at one of the blackjack tables. He could see his brother eyeing him out of the corner of his eye.

"What happen? Are you two fighting?" questioned Brick sarcastically.

"Don't ask," grunted Pike.

Brick's eyes went to his brother's shaking leg. They both had the same tell. Whenever they were pissed and on the verge of opening the floodgates of their anger, they would start with the leg. Brick leaned toward his brother and opened his mouth to speak.

Pike put up a hand to warn him to keep silent. Slowly, Brick clamped his mouth shut. He didn't know what had happened in her room, but he wanted to have his fun before they left the island. He stole one more glance at Pike before he folded on his bet. He had taken enough of the two men's money that were also sitting at the table.

"Here," he offered Pike. "You keep playing for me while I go upstairs. Diamond should be ready for me by now. Will you be ready to go in an hour?"

"Yeah. You'll find me right here."

"You aren't going to; you know?" Whispered Brick. His eyes widened slightly when Pike shook his head, no. With a shrug, he walked off to go seek his pleasure in the bed of one of the girls he usually chose.

"Don't be so sour. I'm sure she'll make it up to you tomorrow," huffed the red-faced man that was perched on the seat; next to the older Asian gentleman, he elbowed.

"It's nice to see she's only putting on a show for us to make us think we have a chance, but we all know, you'll win," chuckled the Asian in a heavy accent.

Pike narrowed his eyes. "What the fuck are you two babbling about?" he growled.

The dealer went deathly still at the anger in his voice. To look at him, he seemed to be just fine, but there was a slow burn that was about to turn into a flame. She knew that there had been a reason why he hadn't been told. When the names on the Mistress's list had been leaked, they all had a hay day gossiping about who made the cut and why others hadn't. They all knew why the handsome, clean cut man that spent hours alone with her but never fucked her wasn't on the list.

"You all need to place your bets," she informed them in an attempt to keep the two, obviously, drunk men from saying too much.

"Does it look like we're playing? Take a damn break," he snapped at the woman. By the time he returned his attention back to the men, they could clearly see that they had fucked up. No longer under the effects of the liquor, they had been pounding steadily since getting on the island, they sobered up under the force of Pike's glare. He flashed the men a creepy smile. "I'd much rather hear what they have to say at the moment," he explained with a wave of his hand as if to tell them to go on. He noticed the nervous looks the two gave the woman. He turned his head slowly just in time to see her mouth the words, *"Don't do it."*

Pike sighed. He took his time while he collected the pile of chips that his brother had amassed and placed them in his coat pocket. "I tell you what, I'll ask you both one more time to explain what the fuck you two are talking about. Or," he stated, slowly as he got to his feet. "I'll shove my hand down your throat and pull the information out that way."

It only took him taking three long strides in their direction for the red face man; that was now drenched in sweat, to start talking. He couldn't afford to return home to his wife all beat up. There was no way he could explain away getting into a fight when he was supposed to be visiting his ailing father in his retirement home.

"Look...look," Mr. Cherry face trembled in a faint voice. He paused, took a deep breath and began to spill all the tea and the biscuits. The dealer rolled her eyes in frustration. Pike glared at her as she turned at sped walked away from the table. He was sure that she was going to warn somebody. That fact made him want to know even more what Cashmere had been hiding from him. The man worked his mouth a few times.

With a sigh, the Asian man interceded, "It's tradition here that the Mistress has to choose a man to father her child," he explained. The man leaped to his feet at the speed Pike closed the space between them. "Hold it! Hold it!" he shouted as he threw up his hands to keep Pike from hitting him in the face. "I...I don't have nothing to do with it, man. I'm just telling you what's going on. It's her time to do her duty."

"How the hell do you know this? I didn't hear a damn thing about it," hissed Pike, taking a step back from the cowardly man. He saw the man's eyes move to his clenched fist.

"Invitations were sent to the men that she was willing to fuc...father her child," he said, as he corrected his choice of words under the intensity of Pike's glare.

Pike was lost in deep thought before he turned away without a word.

"Shit," coughed the red-faced man as he drained his whiskey glass. "Fuck this shit. I had gotten excited to find out that he wasn't invited, but after seeing that," he pointed in the direction of Pike's form disappearing through the archway toward the stairs. "I'll leave it for somebody else. Her cunt; no matter how sweet it will be, isn't worth dying over," he explained.

His Asian friend produced a handkerchief from his pocket, wiped his sweat, and sat back down. "I agree with you buddy, but I'm too damn nosy to give up a good show."

Chapter 2

"Excuse me."

Pike pushed the security guard that was standing at the foot of the stairs out of the way, sending the man against the wall. He took the stairs two at a time. He didn't care about the shouts and the commotion below as he hit the third landing on his way to her door. His hand paused at the door; then he decided against knocking. Taking a firm hold of the gold door knob, he set his shoulder to it and shoved it. The door gave way after he rammed it the second time. Quietly, he closed it behind him. His emerald eyes searched the room for her only to find it was empty. He had never gone beyond the sitting room or the occasional visit to her bathroom that was the only door at the end of the hall to the right. Now, he marched toward the sounds of *J. Cole* that was coming from the hall to the left.

"I see I can add packing to the list of things you do so well."

He might have laughed at the height that she jumped in the air at the sight of him standing in her doorway. His eyes feasted upon her laying in the middle of her bed. He acknowledged the jar of what he assumed to be some type of lotion that he had interrupted her rubbing on her legs. The hem of her light pink satin nightgown gave him an eye full of her thighs before she pushed it back down.

"I thought I would give you a hand in your packing, but I see it's all done, and in record time," he smirked.

"Well, I had done a lot of it yesterday," she stammered as she waved at the many suitcases that were scattered throughout the large room. "How did you get in? I locked the door after-"

"I busted it open," he answered, taking a step into the room.

"You did what?"

"You fucking heard me. I knocked the fuckin door in," he growled.

Cashmere blinked a few times in surprise. There was no denying that he knew.

"I'll be sending you the bill for the door."

Pike lunged forward as she rolled off the bed which caused their bodies to collide. He was like an unmovable wall. She instantly felt her nipples harden against his chest. She attempted to back away, only to be captured in his strong embrace. He knew he shouldn't have done it. His mind was screaming for him to stop while his body was yelling for him to do it. His hands slipped lower to cup her firm ass. Cashmere's feet left the carpet as he pushed her on his stiff cock. He knew what her reaction would be. He had been waiting on it. He lowered his head just as she opened her mouth in protest. His lips moved slowly over her full lips. Her mouth felt just as he had imagined and then some. It was the first time he had ever kissed her. She opened her mouth to let his tongue caress the inside before she joined in with her own.

Her entire body was in tuned with his. She could feel his heartbeat. She could feel the blood rushing to her head and flooding to her pussy. She knew she would blame that rush on her temporary loss of reason. She snaked her arms around his neck. The sound of her moan seemed loud in the still room even to her own ears. She swayed on her feet when he placed her back on the ground. Her heart felt as if it was in her throat. She watched his every movement under hooded lids.

Slowly, he slipped out of his coat. The pricey garment fell to the floor. The alarms went off in her head when his hands went to his shirt. One by one, he opened the buttons on his white cotton shirt.

Don't say it! Oh Lord, please don't say it! a voice in her mind begged. Luckily, she had learned to ignore the impulses that ruled so many women that caused them to give into temptation.

"You have to go," she said as firmly as she could muster. The hard expression on his handsome face only served to make her body cry out even more. She had never seen him this way before. She had always guessed that Pike had a hardness to him. That he had an edge; that he left at the door whenever he was with her. Now that her assumptions were confirmed, it excited her to no end. She had no doubt that he was capable of overpowering her. That he could toss her on the bed and crush her; dominate her in such a tantalizing way that would keep her cumming and moaning.

"I hear your words, but that look in your eyes is saying something completely opposite."

"I don't give a damn about my eyes. I said you have to leave," she demanded in a forceful voice.

"So, you would whether fuck some fat asshole instead of asking me to father your child?"

Cashmere regarded him coldly. If it took hurting him to get out, then so be it.

"*Rich* assholes, darling."

Pike ran his palm over his face to calm himself. "I won't allow it," he said matter of factly.

She tossed back her head and began to laugh only to scream in surprise. She rolled backward over the mattress onto the other side of the bed to put space between them, after he had reached out to grab her.

Her mother held her finger up to her lips to stop the security guard from rushing into the room due to the sound of her scream. They both had been eavesdropping on the two outside the bedroom door. Isobel had made a beeline to Cashmere's apartment after receiving word that he had found out. She felt as if she was watching a soap opera there in the hallway of her daughter's place. She didn't need to see the two to know that the young couple were on the verge of giving into each other. Even out in the dim lit hallway, she could feel the tension. The very air seemed to be electrified with the sexual charge that Cashmere and Pike were given off. She closed her eyes and listened to his hoarse, deep voice.

"Don't talk like that," he commanded.

"Talk like what?"

"Like you're a fuckin whore," snapped Pike.

"I think you've been sucked into an illusion if you thought that I was anything other than a high price bitch."

"God, I would love to be sucked right now," sighed Pike as he rolled his eyes.

"You've forgotten that I'm in the trade of tits and ass," she continued, ignoring his comment. "Yeah, you spend time up here, but you've obviously felt that I'm different from the girl that you tip for sucking your cock before you get on your private plane to take you home. I'm no better than she is."

"Fine, how much to plunge into that gold plated pussy of yours?"

"Get out," she spat.

"Why didn't I get an invitation?"

"I didn't do the picking. My mother did it for me. I couldn't figure out who to ask, so I just watched her. That way I'll know how to do it next time," she lied.

Pike went still as he pinned her with his penetrating gaze. He didn't break contact as the loud voices in the distance reached their ears.

Isobel cursed under her breath. "What the hell happened?"

"I know, and just when it was getting good, too."

"She can't know we were listening; follow my lead," warned Isobel as she tapped the dark skinned Cuban on his arm. She took a few steps back down the hallway and timed the footsteps that were racing their way. At the right moment, she charged into Cashmere's room with her guard, and the others entering a heartbeat later. Her eyes went directly to her daughter and Pike.

"Shit, I think I just nut. Look at them," whispered the Cuban behind her.

She was seeing the same scene he was seeing, and yes, it was intense indeed. Even with all the damn yelling and chaos around them, Pike commanded her daughter's attention.

"Pike, we have to go, Bro. What the hell are you doing? I think I was just set..." rambled his brother until his words trailed off. Brick's hand fell from his brother's arm. He had been pulling on him to get him to move without success. Pike was rooted in place. He stood back while his eyes darted between Pike and a panting Cashmere. Brick could overhear Isobel asking what had happened.

"I'll tell you what happened, this bitch set me up," growled Brick, no longer worried about what was going on with his brother.

Isobel turned her head slowly toward the young girl, Diamond, that had run into the room with the others. Isobel opened her mouth, closed her eyes, and bit down on her knuckled fist, hard. Diamond took a big step back as she threw up her hands in protest.

"Don't tell me that he got caught in the middle. Please, don't tell me that he walked into the *wrong* room?" Isobel's voice had started low. Then it rose to a high pitch by the time she was at the end of her question.

"What? Wait a minute. You knew about this shit? All you mother fuckers were in on this."

"Will you please shut up!" shouted Isobel as her eyes bore into Brick.

"The hell I will. You have no fuckin idea what you just did. When this gets out-"

"So he got in the middle, huh. Oh God," moaned Isobel as she pulled at her black hair in frustration.

"I'm so sorry. I had told him which room to come to, but I think he went to that one out of habit. By the time I got there, well," Diamond shrugged sadly.

The sudden movement from Pike caused everyone to look his way. His steps were slow and purposeful. He rounded the bed that had been blocking him. When he reached her side of the bed, she started to back away from him. A wicked grin formed across his lips. He didn't care if she tried to find an escape. There wasn't one. He positioned himself to ensure she didn't repeat her last maneuver of rolling over on the bed to get away. He just kept coming to Cashmere's dismay. She was sure that he wouldn't try to have his way with a room full of onlookers, but the look on his face made her fearful that he just might. Pike didn't stop his advancement until he had her crushed up against the wall. Even still, he ensured that there was not even enough space for air to fit between their bodies.

His touch was light as he ran his calloused hands over her shoulders, down her arms, to her wrists. Swift, his touch turned rough as he imprisoned her hands in a vise like grip to pull them over her head. He chuckled at her attempt to free herself.

"Your body is so soft," he moaned.

She could hear his loud intake of air as he lowered his head to breathe in her scent. She swallowed hard at the feel of his shaved face while it touched and rubbed against hers.

He could tell by the look in her brown eyes that she wanted him. He had seen that look before many times, but he had respected her wishes in hopes that she would freely give herself to him. He had been willing to wait, but now in light of what she was preparing to embark upon; Pike was done waiting. He was going to be the one, and not just for the task she was seeking men to achieve. He didn't know how, but he was determined to have her then, and every day of his life. His right hand went to her lips. He slowly caressed her full bottom lip with his thumb.

"I think I'll spend an entire hour just feasting on your mouth when we're alone before I suck on your nipples. Oh, I think they're begging to feel my mouth now," he whispered.

She could feel the heat from his green gaze on her harden nipples. The air caught in her throat when he brushed her nipple with his hand. Her loud pants seemed to vibrate off the walls as his hand traveled down her side, to her hip, and to her thigh. Involuntarily, she shifted her stance as she opened her legs. His wicked smile deepened.

"I know I can't take touching you there, Cashmere. I can't wait to, though. I can't wait to lick every fold and taste your pretty pink center. I'm going to fill your kitty with so much cream that it's going to run down your legs and stain your clothes," he promised. He closed his eyes for a second. Then just like the end of a storm, he backed away from her. Without a word, he walked away. No longer having his muscular body to prop her up, her knees buckled, and she slid to the floor, breathless.

Pike approached his wide-eyed, slack-jawed brother. "Didn't you want to leave?" he reminded him.

"Ye...yes," stammered a clearly shocked Brick as he fell in step to disappear out of the room. He waited until they were on the second landing to speak. "I'm in deep shit and now that you're-"

"I don't give a damn about Mom and Dad, and I know you can give two shits about their opinion, too," grunted Pike.

"Yeah, but this might be the straw that breaks the back."

It was something in Brick's voice that made him flatter in his step. A deep frown creased his face. He had never known his brother to worry about the threats their parents rained down on them. Brick always seemed to live above the noise.

"Did you kill a girl?"

"What? Are you crazy?! Where the hell are we going?" Inquired Brick when Pike didn't head for the double French doors, they had entered hours prior. Instead, he headed back towards the casino.

"I'm looking for that cherry faced man that was at the blackjack table," he explained quickly while he paused to scan the room. He slapped Brick on the back and pointed toward the poker tables. He saw the man glance up from his hand to see not one, but two men heading his way. "Then if that's not the case then why you worried?" asked Pike, getting back to his brother's problem.

"Because I think I just fucked the wrong woman," mumbled Brick.

This time, Pike did a double take at his brother's response. He worked his mouth a few times to speak. Then he clamped it shut.

"You're on your own with this one, Brick. I got my own fish I gotta fry."

***

Isobel cleared the room.

"I'm sure you both can't wait to retell the story; just make sure you don't add too much to your version," she hissed before she shoved them into the hallway. She stopped by the bar, poured two glasses of cognac, then strolled back into the room to find Cashmere still on the floor.

"That man will definitely leave a woman weak. Here," she said, shoving the half full glass into her daughter's face.

With shaking hands, Cashmere took the glass and drained it. She leaned forward, snatched her mother's drink and drained that one, as well.

"Care to tell me what that was all about. I thought you two were just good friends," stated Isobel, sarcastically.

Cashmere rolled her brown eyes. This wasn't the first time they had this conversation. "There isn't anything to tell," she promised as she got to her feet, at last, to sit on the edge of her bed.

"Bullshit. I think I heard your ovaries scream. Is that the reason why you didn't invite him?

"I don't see how adding him to the list would have made any difference. Besides, he didn't strike me as the type that would want to father my child."

"Oh, he would, and he would enjoy every lingering second of it, too."

"Not to mention the *other* thing," Cashmere reminded her.

Isobel's eyebrow went up, "Do you think that would? Well, of course, it would with you being highly aroused," she mumbled. "I still think he wouldn't care, Baby. That man *wants* you."

"I know that *Mother!*" she yelled. "That's the reason why I didn't tell him or invite him."

"Then what the fuck am I missing?"

Cashmere sighed and glared at the wall for a second. "Don't you remember what you said to me when I remarked on wanting what Aunt Fran had with Blaze. You warned me that having a man like that would be trouble."

"Ohhhhh," moaned Isobel. "So what's wrong with that?"

"I don't want to be in love. I don't want to have to relive the loss of not being with him every damn day. I'm a fuckin mistress of a broth-"

"Then leave this place," pleaded Isobel.

Cashmere sat back as if her mother had just slapped her. Her almond shaped eyes widened in shock.

"Are you out of your blooming mind? After all, those fuckin years of listening to you preach to me about how running this place was my birthright!" she responded slowly to ensure her every crisply spoken word registered clearly. "Not after watching you scheme and claw your way to the top. Then all the plotting that I did to remove every threat out my way. No fuckin way am I stepping aside. I'm the one that took this place further than anyone before by making sure that every woman here has a future long after their pussy goes dry. Shit, after five years working here, they can leave and live off a king's ransom from their investments and savings. No, it's my duty to-"

"Do you think I care about this palace of ass, cuz that's all it is. We can *both* leave this place, Cashmere. We have money of our own. Why give up what Pike is offering you to-"

"Which is what?" sneered Cashmere as she got to her feet. "All I heard was him offer to fuck me. Isn't that what all the men in this place want to do? I'm a whore. I was born to be a whore. I lived and was raised by whores. I'm not a damn Disney princess. You can't try to narrate my story off of how Kia's or her mother's, or even how Auntie Fran's turned out."

A thin-skinned woman might have been hurt by her daughter's words, but Isobel wasn't. She knew what Cashmere had said was true. However, she was a Mother a well, and like all Mother's, she wanted the best for her child. Even if her baby was too scared to reach for it; she had no problem pushing her ass out of the nest.

"As always, you are level headed enough to see the shit over the trees," replied Isobel with a beaming smile while she collected the empty glasses.

"Should I be worried about whatever happened with Brick tonight?" questioned Cashmere. She jerked back on the covers and climbed into bed.

"No, I don't believe so."

"Humph, I doubt that, but I'll leave it in your capable hands. I have too much shit going own to worry about a silly mix up."

Isobel happily agreed. She walked silently back down the hall and thanked God that her daughter had said that. It was more than just a silly mix up. She had thought that what she was doing would actually help, but it seemed that it only stood to make the poor girl's plot thicken, and this time, maybe for the worse. She shrugged her shoulder while she closed the door to Cashmere's apartment. That young girl was on her own now. Although the girl's scheme had sounded good on paper; there had been too many things that could have created the cluster fuck that had happened that night. It was only because her heart had gone out to the girl was the only reason why she had agreed to help.

Then again, maybe it's divine intervention in disguise, she thought while she walked down the stairs. Brick walking into the room might play out to be a good thing. Hell, he would be much better than the future the girl had been facing.

"Speaking of divine intervention," she smirked as she pulled out her cell phone. She didn't give a damn what Cashmere said; she reminded herself as she waited for the familiar voice on the other end to pick up.

"Yes, Bella."

Isobel rolled her eyes at the voice of her sister. "Why you have to answer the phone like that?"

"Only because you never seem to call unless something is up."

"Now that's not true. I could be calling you to check in or to hear how the babies are doing."

"Bullshit," chuckled Frannie. "But in case that is true, the grandkids are doing great, and so am I, in spite of this clan war shit. I want to gun all those assholes down, but I've been told to hold up for now. So, now that all the shit that I know you didn't really call to hear has been said, what can big sis do for you?"

"Ok, since you asked so damn sweetly, I need your help with Cashmere." Isobel could hear her sister moving around at the mention of her niece.

"What's wrong?"

"She leaves tomorrow for the selection, and there seems to be a new stud that wants to try out for the position."

"You mean a threat?"

"No, not to her safety, but maybe to her future; if everything plays out, would be to her advantage."

"Ok...see, it's been one hell of a day, so cut the crap and tell me in plain English instead of in all these codes, what the hell you want me to do?" grumbled Frannie.

"You know I do that just to piss you off, right," laughed Isobel.

"No shit," chuckled Fran.

"All I want you to do is be present. I want you to see and make the judgment call of if he has more to offer than what all those sweaty bastards there are offering," explained Isobel.

"I understand. So, my little niece isn't smart enough to see what's right in front of her nose. Alright, and if he is..."

"Then I want you to assist him. Can you and Blaze be there?"

"No...not Blaze," sighed Fran. "We are having...issues," mumbled Fran.

"What? Why?" Cried Isobel.

"This possible clan thing has caused me to call on a few old friends, and he didn't like it."

"Well, you aren't married, Fran. Given the life that we have lived, you can't blame the man for being jealous. Who's the guy?" Asked Isobel. She took note of the long pause on Fran's line before her sister spoke.

"Aldo."

Hearing his name made the blood stop pumping to Isobel's heart. Her hand began to tremble on the stair railing.

"You've spoken to him?" she questioned Fran in a faint voice.

"Yes," Fran answered, flatly. She wasn't going to get involved. She had tried. Lord knows she had, but she wasn't going to do a thing if her sister wasn't ready. "Anyway," she stated, shifting the conversation. "I won't have Blaze, but I'll get Levi to come with me. Angie has that baby thing down pat, so I know she won't fall apart for a few days. Text me the place, and we'll be there. I would ask you to tell me who this man is, but for some reason, I think he'll stand out."

Isobel was still frozen on the second flight of stairs long after the phone went dead. She wasn't surprised that Fran had rushed off the phone. Aldo was a bitter wound that had caused them to have a big falling out years ago. It was ironic that that situation which had happened years ago bore a striking resemblance to the one that was staring down at Cashmere. Straightening her shoulders, she felt at peace for calling on her sister to assist her after all. She joined the laughter back at the main level of the brothel. Even though she was there among the girls and the clients, Isobel's mind was on a time long ago.

Chapter 3

Pike slammed the door to his room. All he heard, all morning long, was the shouts and raised voices of his family, and it was starting to get on his nerves. The time registered in his mind after he glanced down at his cell phone. He had been up since the crack of dawn trying up loose ends, gathering his work, making calls, and getting things ready for his month long departure. He dropped the last suitcase by the door. He had decided that if he had left anything behind, he would just have to pick it up when they got to their destination. In his mind, he wouldn't be returning to this place, which was a good thing since his mother was in rare form over Brick.

He ran his hands through his neck length hair as he walked into his closet. Not only had he packed up his room, but he also spoke to his assistant to make sure the home he bought that was a mere forty minutes away was prepared for his return at the end of the month. He wanted to have a place for Cashmere when she returned with him. He was sure that she would like the home. The large six bedrooms, over seventy thousand square foot home was more than enough, but if she wasn't happy with that one, he owned five more in different places she could choose from. Frankly, he didn't give a damn where they lived just as long as she was with him. He was sure that after he got her alone, he would be able to break down her walls.

He emerged from the large walk-in closet to find his valet standing in the room. Pike was sure that the old man was a ninja, due to the way he would appear without making a sound. Not only was the sixty-something-year-old man his valet; he was also a trusted advisor, a friend, and a distant relative. Pike was sure that Dermot kept his father in the loop of the things he did, but, that fact didn't bother him.

"Do you have everything?"

"Are you saying I don't have enough?" beamed Pike. He pulled off his t-shirt, stepped out of his shorts, and let them fall to the ground.

"Hell no, laddie," sighed Demont in his thick Irish accent. "Please say we'll be leaving soon. I love your Mum, but I'm thinking about strangling her arse."

"I'm sorry, but you'll just be trading one bitching for another," warned Pike.

"Oh, but you'll sweet talk that lass until you'll have her purring like a kitten," winked Demont.

"Shit, from your mouth to God's ear," chuckled Pike as he walked into the bathroom.

The hot water on his flesh was a welcome feeling. It helped to calm him. He closed his eyes and was immediately transported back into Cashmere's room. According to what Brick had said, he had created a very balls tightening picture that had left his brother speechless. Now that he could think about it, he knew it had taken all his home training, and every ounce of will power to keep for branding her as his own last night. He had never been that close to her. He had never kissed her, but now that he had tasted her, felt her; he knew he couldn't rest until she was his. He glanced at the droplets of water that was dripping from his stiff cock. He reached down and gripped it. He closed his eyes and took a deep breath. His strong hand stroked it slowly all the way from its root to its mushroom shaped tip.

"Shit," he hissed at the sound of his electric razor dropping into the sink. His green eyes opened with a look of surprise. He turned his head. He could barely make out the form through the frosted shower door, but he was sure that it was his nephew that was perched on the sink counter top. "God Cormac, you scared the living shi...you scared me."

"I'm sorry," the little boy cried.

Pike was just happy that he hadn't been in full swing of pleasuring himself when the boy walked in. That was one conversation the five-year-old wasn't ready for. He paced himself to ensure that by the time he was done with his shower, his throbbing erection had started to go down enough to no alarm the boy.

"You don't have to apologize for scaring me."

"Not that, but for this. I was playing with it, and it slipped," groaned the little boy as he held up Pike's mangled razor. "I'll fix it, Uncle Pike," he offered with big blue-green eyes.

"It's alright," smiled Pike while he toweled down. "Don't tell me all Nana's yelling is getting to you?"

"No way," Cormac promised as he straightened his shoulders to back up his words, only to hunch them over again. "I don't want a Mama, Uncle Pike. I like it being just us men. Why she wants to mess that up with a dumbass woman?" he grumbled.

Pike tossed back his head and laughed. The sound of his deep voice vibrated off the tile walls and floated into the bedroom.

"I'm happy you have a sense of humor. Come out here, boy."

He was still laughing when he strolled back into his room to see that his father had joined the meeting.

"So my room is the hideout," questioned Pike as he began to dress in front of Demont, his father, and Cormac.

"I'm here for *other* reasons," his father, Peter answered slowly. He took note of Pike's eyebrows going up in response.

"If you feel the need," replied Pike while he stepped into his pressed pants.

"Will you be gone long?" Peter started, taking a seat in one of the leather chairs. He glanced at his grandson climbing into Pike's bed to listen.

"About a month."

"Then you'll be back?"

"It's time for me to move out."

"I see," smiled Peter. "In that case, enjoy yourself while you scratch that itch one last time." His smile flattered at the stern expression on Pike's face. He stole a glimpse at Demont sitting next to him.

"It's a lot more than an itch Father."

"I thought so, but you can't blame me for trying."

Pike crossed his arms over his muscular chest. He leaned his shoulder on the wall.

"I would like to leave on a good note, but I don't need your permission. I'm a man of my own means," Pike explained, slowly.

"Oh, son...you have done me very proud. You've been a man for a very long time. Even so, you still gave me respect and let me feel as if I had a say in your life."

"Then is it her color?" questioned Pike.

Peter tilted his head as he regarded his son. The boy actually didn't have a clue. Pike's view of the girl amazed him.

"I know we've never had the conversation before, but I don't give a damn about skin color, which is how I raised you and your brother to be. I'm talking about her background. Your mother would-"

"You say mother, but what about you?" inquired Pike, cutting his father off.

Peter shifted in his chair. He had never seen his son this determined. It was exciting to behold. Pike was smart in finances and business. If he dreamt it, if he planned it, the boy worked diligently until he conquered it. However, this was a whole different battle, which Peter could see that Pike was clearly aware of. There was a level of hardness there that hadn't been before. His son wasn't going to lose.

"It has nothing to with me. I've made my choice, and I'm living with it. Your mother wasn't always the woman she is now. It's the memory of the woman that I fell in love with and the one that I've lost along the way that gives me the strength to stay with her as she is now."

Pike looked at Demont as his uncle nodded his head in agreement. It was true that his mother had undergone a complete transformation after coming to the States when they were still kids. Her desire to fit in with the assholes that she considered friends and neighbors had made her into a bitter, hard pill to swallow; at times.

"All I'm saying is to count the cost," his father finished.

"I've been weighing the cost twice a week for over six months. It's worth every penny," promised Pike.

"Is she now?" asked his father with a smirk.

Pike pushed off the wall, walked to the bed, and began to put on his tank top before slipping into his shirt.

"Cashmere is no different than the whores that I've been fucking since high school or the ones that mother tries to dangle in front of me; in hopes that I'll settle down," Pike pointed out.

"That is true," agreed Peter. "Ah, don't worry. You go and get that girl. Since you said she's what you want, you better not come back empty-handed," demanded Peter as he jumped to his feet. "I was never one that liked being told what to do any fucking way," he spat, waving his hand in the air. "Now, if you excuse me, I need to put your mother in her place."

"Does Cormac have something to be warned about?" inquired Pike.

Peter's hand paused on the silver door knob. He turned back, "I'm a father *and* a businessman. Don't be too long trying to get your lady. I want to have *both* of your weddings this year for a tax write off." Peter walked out the room swiftly to make sure Pike didn't have the chance to ask him to explain. He too didn't give a damn about the wagging tongues of people. Actually; the change of events could be the freedom that the family needed.

***

Pike took his time walking down the cobblestone driveway towards the front door. He smiled at the bright colors of the setting sun that had all but been swallowed up by the approaching night. He was happy that there was a cool breeze coming off of the ocean. He wasn't surprised by the sprawling home in the Keys that was the setting for Cashmere's exclusive party. The place was large enough to allow guests to arrive by boat. He was also aware of the landing pad at the back of the home, but the place was also off the beaten path, too.

He had sent Demont ahead hours ago with their luggage. Pike had wanted to wait until Cashmere had relaxed into playing the role of queen bee before he crashed the party. He didn't know for sure how things were going to play out. To be honest, he really didn't care. If he had to use the gun, that he had holstered under his black dinner jacket, then so be it. Either way, his prize would be leaving with him.

"Sir," cried the surprised man that opened the door. "I can't let you..." His words trailed off at the sight of the invitation that Pike handed over. His look of doubt was written clearly on his face. However, he stepped to the side to let him in. "I don't know how you got that, but that's all I need to cover my ass," said the Afro-Cuban.

"Where is everybody?"

"They're all in the drawing room, but the announcement has been made to go to the dining room," the man whispered in the empty entryway. He quickly closed and locked the door before he bids for Pike to follow him.

"How many showed up?"

"I counted twenty- three."

"Hum, that's not that bad."

"There was only thirty invites sent out, so you can say they *all* want to be the one," the blue, black man explained. For a second, Pike was amazed at how the light reflected off the man's skin.

"Shit," hissed Pike.

"Shit is right, and," the man grabbed Pike's arm to keep him from entering the full room that was buzzing with laughter and conversation. "You see that woman over there?" at Pike's nod, "That's Frannie...Cashmere's aunt. The bitch don't play. From what I know, she's mixed up with the Japanese Mafia, which means if she's here, something is going on. That man she's talking to is a cop or was a cop...I don't know, but you better have a damn good plan is all I'm saying."

Pike reached into his pocket, pulled out a hundred-dollar bill, and pushed the money into the man's rough hands. With a nod, the man stepped into the crowded room with Pike on his heels. Silence overtook the room like a fire to dry wood. One by one, everyone's eyes fell upon the tall elegantly dressed man in all black. The Diamond *P* encrusted cufflinks sparkled in the light. Unlike yesterday night, he kept his neck length free. He reached up and push it back as he strolled across the room. From the moment she came into view, his emerald eyes hadn't left her large brown one. She stood there frozen in time while she took in the heart-stopping vision of him gliding towards her. In his perfectly cut clothing, she could see the muscles in his muscular arms and chest flex. If the people around her were still talking; which they were, she had no idea what was being said. She felt alive, hot, and enraged at the same time which she blamed her sudden feelings of light headiness on.

"What the hell is he doing here?" she grunted.

She glared angrily at the invitation the tall Cuban held in his hand. She snatched it so fast that man wondered if she had cut his fingers with the heavy paper. Quickly, she crumbled it up in her hands and throw it at Pike's head. He ducked just in time, causing it to catch him in the shoulder instead.

"It seems you were able to get invited after all," she snarled.

"As I said before, I'm sure, me not getting one, was just a slight oversight that I fixed immediately," he beamed down into her face.

Her eyes darted around the room. She could already feel the change in the atmosphere. Many of the men there knew Pike. Others know of their very close friendship. For those that were completely clueless, she could see that they were being brought up to date really quick from all the whispering that had begun. Now she was at a new level of frustration at the thought of all the months of preparation, that had gone into day's success, was going down the toilet quickly.

"I hope you didn't straighten out all your soft, beautiful curls on the account of pleasing these men. You never had to do that for me," he said loud enough to make sure his voice carried through the still room. He reached and pushed her heavy black hair back behind her shoulder.

She knew what he was doing. Both his words and his actions were conveying a level of intimacy to the on looking men that wasn't true at all. The both of them knew it, but many of the men in that room had always felt that she and Pike were lovers. She had never seen the need for correcting that assumption, but she realized at that moment; what a mistake, not doing so, had been. She formed a fist.

"Let me stop you before you do that."

She blinked her eyes at Fran. In shock, she glanced down at her still formed fist. Her Aunt was right. Hitting Pike would do nothing but give her a stinging hand and make her look like a fool in front of the few men that seemed to still want to stick around.

"I'm going to get you for this," she hissed at Pike before she began to walk past him.

"Don't make me wait," he moaned as he reached down and rubbed her ass when she passed by for all to see.

Both Fran and Levi laughed. They had wondered who the threat would be. Now that he was here, they could see why Cashmere was worried. Not only was the man good looking, but he also had confidence that was borderline arrogant.

"A drink?"

"I could use one, yes."

"You can be one big asshole," chuckled Levi when the man just stared at them as if he expected for the two of them to get his drink.

"I'm really not that big of one. I'm just trying to understand why her Aunt is here?" admitted Pike with a wink. He walked over to the bar to pour himself a drink. He kept his eyes on Cashmere while she went back to talking to the fifteen or so guests that hadn't excused themselves and left. She looked like a flame in the red gown that clung to her every curve to trail behind on the ground. The plunging neckline gave all the men and eye full of her breast.

"We're here because of you, of course," replied Fran. She liked the fact that he wasn't taken back by her words. Instead, he actually seemed amused. His emerald green eyes seemed to sparkle. The man was tall and handsome with his clean cut looks. However, Fran saw something else too. There was a dangerous element to him too. She didn't think that he was dangerous in the definition that she was used to, but there was something there that was exciting to any warm blood women that was intoned. There no questioning the reason why her niece had kept him from the list of suitors. The man put all the others in the room to shame. "Have we met?" she questioned.

"No. You have a way about you that would have made me remember."

"As do you," remarked Fran as her eyes appraised him openly. "You obviously have people on the inside that's rooting for you; against my niece's wishes."

He downed his drink, placed it on the bar, and examined the woman. He had no problem seeing the resemblance in her and Cashmere's mother. They both had the same lips, nose, and eyes that shone with cleverness. He had a hard time figuring out her age because she looked so young, too damn young to be honest. Her youth wasn't just in her face either, it was her entire body, he noticed as he repeated her act of looking her over. Even in the plain, tight black dress she was wearing, the woman looked good. She made the clothes, not the other way around.

"Are you and your friend with me, too?"

"Could be...at least that's why Isobel asked us to be here. She wanted us to see if you had the balls to bring home the prize or if you were just another one hoping to tap that honey pot."

"I have the balls, and the entire package to back up all the shit I put down. Including making Cashmere forget all about going back."

"It looks like this man has a plan to me. Shit, why the hell did I even come then," smirked Levi. "I'm telling you now, that it takes a strong man to marry on of these women. I thought I had an iron will, but they will test your fuckin patience."

"Hold up now. You don't say that until *after* we have him on lockdown," joked Frannie.

Pike felt the tension ease from his body hearing that he had been given the help he needed to put his plan into action.

"Ok, how is this going to go down?" asked Levi.

**

Cashmere had been annoyed at the presence of her Aunt and Angie's husband, Levi showing up, but now that she saw them talking to Pike, she decided to thank her mother after all. Whatever they had said to him must have done the trick. During dinner, he was the laid back, funny, and engaging man that she was used to spending time with. He quietly listened to the conversations that went on around the large wooden dinner table. He sipped the wine under his hooded lids throughout the entire time while the other men fought for her attention. She should have been happy. However, his manner seemed to come off as cocky.

Or is it that he doesn't have his head up your ass is pissing you off? The voice in her mind said.

She doubled her efforts to get a rise out of him to the point that she leaned over to entice the men with her full breast. He narrowed his gaze as if to warn her to stop it before he went back to talking to Levi. The fact that she did as he had said made her mad, too. This wasn't at all how she has thought this night would go. He might appear to be at ease, but she was a bundle of nerves with him being there. Of course, she was happy that he had found a way to crash the weekend. She knew she would never forget the opposing image he had created entering the room. However, that was all he had done. Why wasn't he as forceful as he had been the other night? Why wasn't he as bold as he had been when he had arrived? Had he just thrown in the towel?

The fact that he's here say otherwise, dummy, the voice promised her.

The thought that he was still going to try to get his way excited her to no end. Although she knew that she was playing with a loaded gun, she couldn't resist. She felt as if she was walking on air as she strolled up the flight of stairs to her room. Many of the men had all left for the evening with hopes of returning in the morning to be picked to stay while she sent the others packing.

"Ah, Auntie," she laughed upon opening her door to find the woman in her suit.

"I think the night went great, Honey," beamed Frannie, handing Cashmere a cup of tea. "Were you expecting someone else?" asked Fran. She had seen the way Cashmere's eyes had scanned the area of the room as if she had been looking for someone.

"No, no," she lied, taking the cup from her hands. She took in Fran's strange attire. No longer was she in the black dress from earlier. She had traded them for a pair of black leather leggings and a see-through black shirt. "Are you going somewhere?" she questioned, eyeing the black combat boots she was wearing.

Frannie shrugged her shoulder. She pondered if she was going to have to use the knockout spray that Levi had given her if Cashmere didn't ingest enough of the sleeping pills she had crushed in the tea. Luckily, her niece took a large enough swig to put her fears to rest.

"Actually, we're *both* going somewhere. I'm going home, and you're going with him," explained Fran.

A deep frown formed on Cashmere's face as she turned slowly just in time to see Pike walk out of the shadows.

"What the fuck?" she started only for her Aunt's casual response to stop her from cursing the roof down.

"She won't be giving you too much trouble. She gulped down enough to make sure she'll be out for a while," Fran said with a deep eye roll. "Look at her, already swaying on her feet."

"Did you get her clothes ready?"

"Enough. They're over there," pointed Fran to the suitcase Cashmere now saw sticking out behind the couch.

"I can't believe this," slurred Cashmere.

Fran closed the space between them. "Oh, don't play the damsel card, baby. It's so beneath you. I saw the look of disappointment in your eyes when it was me in your room and not him," whispered Fran in her ear. She took a step back to glare into her face. The cup Cashmere had been holding finally fell from her numb hands causing the remaining tea to spill onto the hardwood floor.

Cashmere's heavy eyes widen due to the two hard slaps her Aunt laid across her face.

"Now listen to me," commanded Fran shaking the girl. "I know you have to curse and pretend to be upset, but don't be a bitch. You don't want to waste the time you've been given. Just focus on you, and this man; that's obviously is the shit cuz we're helping him. Damn, she's going...somebody!" shouted Frannie.

Instantly, Pike was there to push Fran out of the way and catch Cashmere when she passed out. Gently, he held her limp body in his arms. All three of them headed for the stairs to the main floor, and then to the waiting car that would be taking Pike and Cashmere to the private plane that he had arranged to fly them away. He gave Fran a piece of paper that had the location they could find them and his contact information. Levi and Fran watched the car drive away before they turned to go to the docks. With their mission completed, there was no longer any need for them to stay.

"Well, I guess your break won't be that long after all," chuckled Fran. "What the hell is that?" she whispered in awe. The seaplane that had brought them to the house was there as she had expected. It was the other craft that sent a chill down her spine. It was nothing like she had ever seen before in her life. It seemed to levitate a whole ten inches off the water. It was clearly something that was secret, and not seen by the masses. It looked more alien than human.

"That's my ride. A friend of mine called me to do him a favor, so this is where we part ways. But I didn't think I would be riding in this," explained Levi, a bit hesitantly.

"What kind of favor?"

Normally, Levi would have kept what he had been told to himself, but it was something in her voice that made him break the code he held to since his years in Special Ops.

"Have you seen a craft like that before?" he asked while he took a step closer. He wanted to get a view of her face that had been hidden by the shadows of the night. He needed to confirm what his ears was picking up in her shaky voice.

"Where are you going, Levi?

"I'm going to LA to check on something for a friend," he lied. "He wants someone to verify a medical, biological finding that he had been working on for a corporation. It's real top secret for a Mr. Tsugumi Ohba."

He didn't have to ask if she had heard of the man. The lack of color in her face was all he needed to see. His training was telling him that there was a lot more to this story than a friend from his past calling him out of the blue. He wondered if she was the connection.

"Did my name come up when you were talking to your friend?" she gulped.

He had never seen her in such a state. Fran always carried herself as if she had the upper hand, but now, he could actually see beads of sweat on her forehead. What he had heard in her voice before, he now realized was pure fear.

"Why would he? You must be the shit, Fran. Only a handful of people can boast to seeing the man."

"I never said I saw him," she snapped.

"Are you going to stand here and bullshit me? I need to know what I'm stepping into," he stated in a controlled voice.

"The man's a myth. People make up stories about him as if he's a non-aging beast," she answered as she tried to turn to walk to the plane.

Levi's hand shot out to stop her. "If that's the case, then why the hell are you trying to run away?" He took a step back at the force she pulled away.

"At times, Levi you need to say, no. If this guy...whoever the fuck he is *was* your friend; he wouldn't even have cast Ohba shadow over you. Go back to Angie, and *do not* mention that you told me about anything," she suggested. She marched without looking back at a confused Levi. Even though she had told him to leave it alone, she knew that he wouldn't. Levi was a man of his word. If that didn't cause him to get aboard the freaky aircraft, the detective in him would. The same curiosity in him that had almost gotten Angie, Luna, and him killed would take him into a place, and a world that could have only came out of a fiction book.

She strapped herself into her seat with shaking hands while she shouted to the pilot to take off. Her mind went back to the two times she had seen Mr. Tsugumi Ohba. Once when he saved her life as a kid. Then one more time, when he arranged a meeting with her twenty-one years later when she was in her thirties. It was that second visit that had made her a true believer.

Chapter 4

"You need to eat something."

Cashmere glared at the plate that Pike placed in her lap. Silently, she picked it up and placed it on the table without touching any of the food, just like she had done with all the others he had tried to tempt her with on the eight-hour flight. Luckily, she had slept during the first half. Even still, she was ready to get the hell off the flying tin can that was taking her to God knows where? She had stopped asking him their destination thousands of mile back. Since he was going to be tight lip, she had decided to do the same by ignoring him completely.

"So it's going to be a hunger strike then" he sighed. "I'm going to miss all that fine ass when you begin to waste away," he joked.

He snatched up the plate. He brought the folk to his mouth slowly. His tongue licked the tender roasted meat on the fork. He didn't know if her eyes were lingering on his mouth because of the suggestive act he was doing or because of the of the loud rumbling of her stomach. He bit the meat, allowing the juices to moisten his bottom lip before he tossed back his head to chew the food.

"You're a fuckin asshole," she growled. She looked out the window while he laughed. "How much longer?"

"About forty minutes," he answered while he handed the full plate back to the stewardess.

"Then can you tell me where we're going? It isn't as if I'm going to jump from the plane."

"I know. I just wanted to piss you off by not telling you."

Cashmere tilted her head as she pinned him with her narrowed gaze. "You're doing really good on that front."

"I'll tell you, but first, you have to change. The weather has a dampness to it that I'm sure you aren't used to," he warned.

Her brown eyes widened as she took in his change of clothes. She hadn't looked at him long enough to notice that he had changed out of his dinner attire to the acid washed jeans that hung low on his hips and the firm fitting navy ribbed long sleeve shirt he was wearing. Her eyes went to his shoes that looked like heavy hiking boots. She wondered if everything he wore would make her want to tear it off in a fit of lust?

"I didn't pack for cold weather."

Pike held up his hand, walked away, only to return carrying a duffle bag. "I picked this up for you myself," he smiled.

The thought of him walking into a store to buy her clothes made the butterflies in her stomach flutter. Planning had gone into her kidnapping, she acknowledged. Not wanting him to know how his actions excited her, she snatched the bag from his hand.

"Call me if you need help," he called after her before she slammed the bathroom door. He checked his watch to see how much time they had left in the air. He hoped that the preparations he had asked for would be there. He laughed in the empty room when he imaged the look on Cashmere's face when she saw what he had in store for her. If she was going to play the bitch card, he had his ways of breaking her. She was used to calling the shots, but she was at his mercy. He was going to put just enough pressure on her to make her as yielding as the meat he had just eaten. He closed his eyes and shifted his thickening cock. He couldn't wait till the cat and mouse game that she was playing would finally come to an end.

He jumped at the sound of the bathroom door opening. Pike had no doubt that the clothes he had provided for her would fit to perfection. He had over six months to size her up. The skinny jeans stretched over her hips, hugging her ass, and fit her toned thighs just right. He wasn't planning on doing it, but the vision of her walking towards him got the best of him. He met her the few remaining steps and pulled her into his arms. He could tell by the stiffening of her body that his actions had caught her off guard.

"I'm happy to see that everything fits," he admitted in a deep voice as he towered over her. Her shortness always excited him. She was so small compared to him, in spite of the fact, that she was thick and shapely. His strong hands dropped to cup her ass cheeks.

She had to resist the urge to stand on her tip toes so she could grind on his erection that was pressing on her stomach. She had never touched his dick, but she was tempted to do so at that moment; to measure its thickness and length. Even still, from what she could feel, she was sure that she wouldn't be disappointed. She lifted up her arms to bring attention the sweater that was two times her size. The sleeves swallowed up her hands.

"You'll be happy that it's big," he promised.

"You haven't told me where we're going," she reminded him in a dry tone that didn't show the lust that was bubbling in her pussy.

Pike hid the annoyance he experienced from her attitude behind a fake smile as he released her.

"Ireland." He gave her a second to process her shock.

"Why?"

"Because I wanted you in a place where I could have you all to myself. Since you'll be having my baby, I can tell our son or daughter how it was conceived in my ancestral home."

"You're Irish? Well, that explains the ginger hair," she waved. "You must have left when you were young."

He didn't let the fact that she didn't correct him go to his head.

"I was thirteen when we left. My Mom wanted her sons to be free of the accent, so she hired tutors to help us get rid of it, but after a few days of being here, I'll slip in and out of it with ease," he explained while he took her temperature a few degrees higher with his heated gaze.

Fifteen minutes later, Cashmere pulled the heavy wool jacket he gave her close as she rode silently next to him in the *Range Rover*. The weather was more than damp. It was downright cold. However, he seemed not to be bothered by it in the least. She took in the city streets of the mid-size town outside of Dublin, Ireland. It was just as the Travel Channel had portrayed it to be. It was like taking a step back in time. The streets were smaller than in America. The concrete buildings in the city looked as if they had been there for years, but not in a decaying way. The architecture had an old world charm that was quaint, close together, and very bright and colorful in some places. Unfortunately, the ride through the town was over in a blink of an eye to be replaced by the lush greenery of the countryside.

"That was quick," she said when he made a right turn into an open gate. He drove slowly down a bumpy dirt road which took them deeper into the woods. "What's the horse for/" she inquired confused.

Pike got out the car, ignoring her. The bright smile he had at seeing Demont by the horse vanished when he caught sight of the man's swollen black eye. Demont pulled Pike in for a bear hug.

"I see you managed alright," said Demont as he tilted his head toward the idling vehicle.

"It took nothing short of a village, but yeah. So, they didn't waste any time, huh?"

"No boy, they didn't. They caught me at the pub. You know how quick talk is around here."

"They got you good," chuckled Pike. "How is she doing?" asked Pike, seriously.

"As beautiful and as reasonable as ever. I swear, only the women have the brains in that family. You what gonna to happen?" warned Demont.

"Shit, I rather it be them than her," confessed Pike as he thumbed in the direction of the car with an eye roll.

Demont let out a loud laugh. "That bad," he beamed while he hit Pike on the back. "Oh, I'm going to enjoy watching this. Some might say this is payback, you know," he winked with his one good eye.

"Bullshit, this is-" Pike stopped talking at the sound of the car door opening.

"Me thinks your break is over, son," chuckled Demont.

Cashmere was tired of sitting in the car while the two of them laughed it up. Pike shouldn't be happy while she was still focused on sticking it to his ass. She marched toward them. She recalled seeing the salt and peppered man once or twice when Pike and Brick came for their bi-weekly visits to the brothel.

"Cashmere, this is my Uncle Demont."

She gave the man's outstretched hand a firm shake.

"Welcome to Ireland, young lady. I'm looking forward to getting to know you," remarked Demont.

"I would say thank you, but seeing how this wasn't my idea..." she let her words trail off at the side eye the man shot Pike. She glanced at Pike and took note of his clenched jaw. She didn't want people to think she was a bitch. Her frustration was directed at Pike, not this man or anyone else. Just like that, the sun parted through the clouds when she gifted the older man a natural, bright smile. She saw the wary expression cross Demont's rugged, yet handsome face, by her sudden change.

"As I was saying, in spite of the change in my plans, I tend to enjoy it. I've never been to Ireland, but from what I've seen so far, it reminds me of the books I've read with Druids and magical creatures."

"Oh, aye...we have many things like that here. I can tell you many stories."

"Hell, maybe I'll get to find myself a pot of gold," she chuckled.

"I think we need to get going," mumbled Pike. It pissed him off that she would be sweet to Demont, yet treat him like shit. He started to guide her towards the awaiting horse.

"That's really rude, Pike," she said with force sweetness.

Demont's smile deepened. He knew what was going on. The narrowed eyed expression that Pike gave the girl was priceless. Demont hadn't prayed in years, but he was going to thank the Blessed Mother for making him come along on this trip.

"What happen to your eye?" she inquired while she touched the side of Demont's face.

"The old man walked into a tree. It's easy to do out here. Now come on," Pike hissed, taking hold of her hand. This time, he dragged her behind him to the horse. He didn't spare Demont another glance as the laughing man walked to the *Range Rover*, got in, and began to back up.

"Why are we taking this horse?" she questioned. Honestly, she was thrilled by the gesture.

"Damn, you change like the wind. What happen to the bright smile, the winks, and the touching?" he mumbled as he positioned her next to the horse.

"I have no beef with that man, and I can mount without your help," she informed him.

Pike bit his lip while she slipped her foot into the stirrup, took hold of the saddle, and pulled herself up. She gifted him with a snooty grin from above.

"I'm not surprised that you would be good at riding on top."

"I've never had a complaint."

He paused at her response. "If you don't want me to treat you like a whore then you need to check yourself," he warned in that cool way that sent a chill down her spine. He got on behind her, pulled her back against him, and sent the horse running up the hill. The crisp air bit at her brown face, but she didn't care. He was happy to hear her laugh as the large chestnut colored horse picked up speed, tossing up the moist soil under his big hooves.

"Oh my Lord," she sighed in wonder. On the top of the hill, he commanded the horse to stop. The great beast pranced while Cashmere admired the patchwork of different shades of green of the land below. At their vantage point, she was able to see for miles of the flat lands, the forest, fields, what appeared to be the remains of a stone building, and large pond before the land went back up into an even larger hill.

"Is the ocean near here?"

"It's on the other side of that hill a few miles away, which is where we're going. Hold on," he replied. She didn't have to. Pike snaked his strong arm around her as they plunged down the hill. She leaned back onto his muscular chest. She breathed in the air, the smells of nature, and a clean, sensual scent that was his alone. She let her hand gravitate to his thigh. She marveled at the feel of his muscles under her fingertips as they contracted with the gentle signals he gave the obedient animal.

Pike leaned forward and nestled his face next to hers. Wanting to take advantage of the closeness, he slipped his hands under her oversize sweater.

"What the hell?"

"You don't want my hands to freeze, do you?" he cried, mockingly. His free hand stroked her stomach as the other moved upward to cuddle her breast.

"What are you doing?" she asked. She noticed the huskiness in her voice.

"Searching for a warm spot," he spoke in her ear. Knowing that he had her trapped, he pulled down on her lacy bra to free the firm mound. He cupped it in his large hand before he began playing with her nipple. "I should have had you ride facing me so I could suck on your breasts," he said.

"I'm guessing this is why you chose the horse."

He smiled into her silky hair. She could pretend to be unmoved his actions, but he could hear the catch in her voice.

"How long are you going to act as if you don't want me, Cashmere?"

"I-," she started only to let out a scream when she felt him lifting her from the saddle. He had moved so fast. In a blink of an eye, he had picked her up, turned her around, and placed her on his lap facing him.

Pike didn't care if she put up a fight or not. He wanted to see with his eyes what his hand had just felt.

"Shouldn't you be leading the horse?" she questioned, worried.

"He knows his way back," he moaned as he positioned her better against his throbbing cock. "God, I can't wait to feel you."

"Are you so sure you will?"

"Don't fuckin push me, Cashmere. I'll give you your time to whine, but I will be wetting my dick in that juicy pussy of yours and watching you cum. Do you scream or do you whimper?" he asked as he tilted his head.

His green eyes had deepened in color. She couldn't take her eyes off of him. His 5'oclock shadow had given his face a ruggedness she hadn't seen before, but she found sexy as hell. She licked her lips slowly. He traced the path of the tip of her tongue across her bottom lip with his calloused thumb.

"Open your mouth," he commanded, softly.

The sound of his deep voice. The glazed over look of lust in his eyes combined with his dominating attitude was too much for her. She parted her full lips. She drew his thumb up to the knuckle into her mouth and began to suck hard. Pike watched her from under hooded lids before he removed his finger. He placed his palm on her back and pressed her forward.

"Give me your tongue."

Once again, she opened her mouth for him to ravish her mouth. Neither one cared about that they were trotting through the countryside. All that mattered at the moment was the feelings of warmth and deep desire that were boiling within each other. Cashmere ran her hands through his hair. She wanted to get closer. She wanted to let him do all the things he had promised. She wanted what he had brought her there for.

Pike's hands slid into the waist of her pants to nettle her ass. Her hands moved to the hem of his sweater. He moaned when her soft hands came in contact with his chest. She followed the ripples of his abs, to his rock hard pecks, then she slipped them under his arms to run her nails up the sides of his back.

"My God," he whispered against her wet lips. "I've dreamt of having you. Now, that I have you, I'm never going to let you go."

"At least for the next thirty days," she responded. Cashmere opened her eyes at the stiffening of his body. She blinked in surprise.

"I will be-"

"You need to turn back around," he informed her sternly, cutting her off.

Now facing forward, she tried to finish her statement a few times, but he continued to cut her off by pointing out things along the countryside to the point that she gave up. She knew he was aware of what she was trying to say. That was enough for her, for now.

"Are we almost to your home?" she sighed. Her inner thighs were beginning to hurt from the rubbing of the saddle.

"You'll see it when we get to the top of this hill."

"So, where does your land start?"

"We've been on it from the second we left the town. Actually, that town was part of the land, but somewhere along the line, it was deeded over. Our land is a total of fifteen hundred acres, and..." he paused. "It also includes that."

"What the fuck," she hissed in awe when the crest of the tower came into view. Pike held the horse to give her a moment to process all she was seeing.

"A got damn castle. When you said ancestral home, that's what I expected...a *home*," she cried.

His clicked the horse into motion. "I know it isn't Hogwarts," he chuckled.

"It's more like Beauty and the Breast," she grumbled. Getting serious, "It's breathtaking, Pike. I might be pissed to be here, but it's all very overwhelming. I had no idea your family was *this* rich."

"Well, we were, then we weren't. We can trace our roots all the way back to the only King of Ireland, King Brain Boru, who ran things over a thousand years ago. Then later, someone in the family tree gambled and drunk everything away. My father was determined to restore his family's greatness, and that's what he did. Although he's the *Lord* of the land, it's his clan that lives and farms the land."

She was silent as she took in the impressive gothic site in front of her. A manicured lawn led up to a paved driveway before a few steps that went to a heavy wooden and iron door. The dark blue limestones of the castle stood proudly in the setting sun. A large lake sat off to the right of the place to disappear behind it to feed into smaller waterways. She counted the four linking irregular castellated turrets. She focused on the coat of arms that was displayed on the northern porch.

"How big is it?"

"Well, I don't like to brag, but it's pretty big," he laughed at the stiff elbow she gave him in his ribs. "Oh, you meant Dromoland Castle," he teased. "It's twenty-eight bedrooms, and over seventy thousand feet, so, of course, there's a lot more rooms than that," he explained.

She could see the pride in his expression as he showed her around the massive castle. She wouldn't have mind. She was actually excited, but the time change was starting to catch up with her which was strange; after her sleeping pill induced coma. After she hid her fourth yawn, Pike took pity on her by showing her to their rooms. She leaned on the wall in the thin hallway to catch her breath. It seemed as if they had been climbing flight after flight of stone spiral stairs with no stop in sight. Pike turned back, picked her up in his arms, and forged onward up the last two flights to the tower. He kicked open the door and crossed her over the threshold. He stood in the middle of the room as he smiled down into her face.

"Welcome," he whispered, dropping a kiss on her cheek.

Cashmere wiggled out of his arms. "I'm not staying with you, Pike. You won out the other candidates, but after I've gotten what I need, I'm heading back."

"I can see our babies running through this house. Can't you?" He asked while he walked passed her.

"No, I can't because they won't be here. Are you dumb and deaf?" she shouted, frustrated.

Pike swirled around and marched back toward her. He rose his hand, then brought it back down to his side. "You make me want to beat your arse, Cashmere." He sighed while he ran his hand over his face. "I'll give you a few days to work through this stage you're in, but it's only so much of this shit from you I'm willing to take," he warned.

"Or what?"

She fought to stand her ground as he pinned her with a narrowed gaze. He tilted his head. "Your mother or your staff isn't here to keep me from spanking you, Cashmere. I had to pull strings to get you *into* Ireland, which means you can't leave without a passport. So, unless you have one shoved up that ass of yours, you can't go home without me," he sneered.

She bounced back and forth on her feet while she tried to think of an equally threatening comeback, but she knew she had no cards to match his. He was wise to have gotten her on his turf, in his home, with his family and friends.

"I'm hungry," she grumbled as she brushed past him.

He wanted to point out that she was because due to her stubbornness, but he was happy with his victory. He placed his hands in his pants. His eyes watched her every facial expression to see if she liked his rooms or not. Unlike the other rooms, his family had chosen, he wanted to keep the old world feel. He didn't want his place to look like a hotel room on the inside. Instead, he commissioned for handmade ceiling to floor tapestries to be hung on the stone walls. The fabrics pictured depicted great battles, dragons, festivals, fairies, and a racy one of what could only be described as a drunken party that turned into a wild orgy. An oversized bear skinned rug sat under his large four post bed that seemed to draw her eyes. Another rug was placed in front of a huge fireplace to divide the room into a sitting area. The furniture was a mixture of cherry wood, leather, and very masculine.

"What's in there?"

"One room acts as a closet and an office. The other one is the bathroom."

Not really interested in exploring the closet/office, she walked into the bathroom. She liked the way the room flowed with the main one. A large wooden barrel bathtub stood in the middle of the bathroom. There was no shower to speak of. If it weren't for the shiny, copper fixtures on the tub, she would have wondered if buckets had to be carried in to fill it. The bathroom was finished off with a copper pipe exposed sink, and a toilet that was hidden behind a hanging tapestry.

"You did an excellent job, Pike," she smiled as she walked back into the room. She went to the window and glanced out over the garden that seemed to stretch out for miles. "No T.V.?" she asked as an afterthought.

He walked over to the foot of the bed, touched a button on the side of large foot board, then took a step back as a concealed flat screen began to rise, slowly.

"Anything else?" He smiled.

Cashmere shook her head, sleepily. She stumbled over to the bed, sat down, and pulled off her boots. She got to her feet; then she looked at him sheepishly before she shrugged her shoulders.

"I hate sleeping with pants on. They make my legs itch," she explained.

Pike watched her while she stripped out of her pants. He had felt the string of her thong when he had warmed his hands in her pants. Now he was able to see the white, lacy item. His gaze scanned her lower half. He felt his cock leap to life as it begged to be released from his pants. Without shame, he gripped it hard as he bit his bottom lip.

"Are you against sleeping in that sweater, too?" he questioned in a deep voice.

Cashmere glanced up from stepping out of her pants. She knew he hadn't left the room, but the vision he created in front of her, holding his dick made her instantly wet. Her eyes focused on his hand. Slowly, she pulled the hem of the thick, oversized sweater up her body. She heard him moan while he shifted his cock. The jeans and the distance were making it hard for her to see just how thick or long his dick actually was. In one fluid movement, she pulled the sweater off and dropped it to the ground. Her breath caught in her throat when he took a step toward her only to stop.

He noticed the redness in her eyes. "I'll let you sleep," he mumbled before he turned away.

She frowned and cursed under her breath after he left the room.

"What the fuck is wrong with him?" she hissed into the empty room. Annoyed, she jerked back the covers and slid into bed. The innocent pillow took a few of her hard punches before she sighed.

I'm sleepy anyway. I'm sure he'll try tonight, she thought with a smile.

She'll be rested and ready. Cashmere moaned as she rubbed her throbbing pussy. She couldn't wait to fuck Pike. She had wanted him ever since she had seen his well manner self all those months ago. There were just times that a woman knew that a man was going to be an amazing lover. That he would fuck her in a way that he would be permanently etched into her brain. It was something in the way he looked at her, touched her, and spoke that made her feel that he was practiced and in control, even in the bedroom. She had no problem being dominated by Pike. As a matter of a fact, she wanted him to. The way he commanded for her to open her mouth made her want to open a whole lot more than that to him. She wanted to be taken into hand. She wanted to give him control, and she knew that he wouldn't do anything to hurt or disrespect her while she was in his control. She had no doubt that his feelings for her ran deep. Much deeper than the friendship that they had been indulging in. She always wondered why he never asked for more? If he had, she knew she would have given it, and since he never did, she damn sure wasn't going to look the fool by asking.

Well, isn't that what he's asking for now; more? The voice in her head pointed out.

She rolled over and closed her eyes tight. Yeah, he was asking for more; too damn much more. She wouldn't have minded an affair on *her* terms, but not what he wants now. How could she give up what had taken over twenty-seven years to obtain, since the day of her birth? This was what her mother had always wanted. It's what *she* has wanted. It sounded as if she was trying to convince herself more than anything. She had never in her wildest dreams considered that her life would be different from what it had been. She took a deep breath to still her pounding heart. It didn't take long after that before she was fast asleep.

Chapter Five

Six hours later, Cashmere was a pacing ball of energy. She had woken up in an empty room with a raging fire to keep her warm. After she had taken a long hot bath, she got dressed in one of her silk nightgowns and navigated her way back downstairs to the kitchen. She had been happy that the food in one of the two side by side stainless steel refrigerators was appealing to her. She piled the plate with potatoes and roast beef, and if the meat was actually something other than roast beef, she didn't care. It tasted delicious. She sat in the quiet kitchen while she ate. Every so often, her eye strayed to the clock that was mounted on the wall by the china cabinet. It was well after midnight, and Pike still hadn't returned.

She sat back and sighed. Her Aunt had warned her about playing the bitch card for too damn long. She, herself, was well aware how being difficult with a man for too long could spell the ruin of a relationship. In spite of the fact that she was pissed, she knew deep down that she was happy that Pike was going after what he wanted, which was her. Now as she walked through the impressive home, she experienced a ping of disappointment. She had thought he would have taken advantage of their first night together.

"You're being silly," she coached herself. "Stop being a whiny ass punk and get what you want."

She quickened her steps through the house and up the torturous flights of winding stairs to her room. A wicked smile formed on her face which grew with each step that it took her closer to the man she knew would be in bed waiting for her. Unfortunately, fate was having a laugh at her expense because when she opened the door, she found herself again in an empty room. Anger exploded in her as she slammed the wooden door.

Where the fuck is he? the voice in her mind screamed.

She stomped across the room and threw herself down in the leather chair before the fire. Her leg bounced up and down before she got to her feet, only to slump back down in the chair a few seconds later. She wanted him, damn it. Isn't that why he had brought her here, so where the hell was he? Where was all that talk about keeping her full and satisfied? Needing something to do, she snatched up the book that sat on the table between the two chairs. She turned the colorful pages forcefully until she realized that it was a photo album. Quickly, she went to the beginning and this time, took her time scanning the pages that was filled with his childhood memories.

Even as a child, Pike was cute as was his brother. The pages were filled with pictures of them as babies. Then photos of them romping around the countryside and in a humble looking home. A frown creased her brow when a pattern began to form. From the time that Pike was probably in his early teens, an attractive blonde began to show up more and more in the photos.

"Maybe it's a cousin," she mumbled under her breath as she continued.

Do cousins hold hands while they walk? The voice in her head wondered.

"I'm sure some do," she answered herself slowly.

However, three pages later, she heard the voice in her mind say, *I told you so.*

Cashmere brought the book up to her face while she sat up to use the light of the fire to see. He had to be in his early twenties. The scenery was picturesque. It was obvious from the stamp on the right corner of the photo that it was done by a professional.

Like a wedding announcement, maybe?

She might have told that voice in her mind to, shut up, but the picture of him sharing tongue with the blonde confirmed it all. Swiftly, she went back to where the girl started to appear in the album. This time, she viewed each photo in a whole new light. The two of them had known each other for a very long time. The theme of the girl popping up went throughout the rest of the book. Slowly, she put the book down on the table.

She wondered if she really knew Pike. Yeah, they talked and shared time together over the last few months, but she was aware how people tell a little and keep a bit too. Hell, even she didn't tell him *everything* about her life. There were some topics that they had both shied away from because neither one had wanted to cross the line. She got up, turned on the T.V, laid down in bed, and did her best to wait for him to return. It was well after four in the morning before she stopped fighting sleep.

PURSUED

Later that day was no better. She only caught glimpses of him as he went about his business with his family and friends. He would smile, ask her how she was doing, then be off to go about his way. She spent the day with Demont, who showed her around the castle and the gardens. He kept her laughing with his stories of the myths of the lands, and of Pike's childhood. She wanted to ask him about the chick in the photos but decided just to wait until later that night to ask Pike herself. However, she did ask about Pike's whereabouts.

Demont kept a straight face as he pretended not to know anything. He was happy to see that the lass was out of sorts in wonder of where the boy had been last night. Of course, he could have told her, but he chose to let her stew a bit.

"Well, you know how it is. The boy has some catching up to do," he winked.

Cashmere narrowed her eyes and clamped her mouth tight. Her anger only grew as the day turned into night, and Pike had made no attempt to see her. She no longer gave a damn about playing games when the clock read eleven- thirty on his nightstand next to the bed. Demont or somebody was going to tell her where the fuck he was. With determined steps, she marched through the house toward Demont's room that was on the other wing of the home. She slowed her step on the landing that overlooked the main hall when a woman's laughter rang out. Cashmere's mouth hung open at the sight down below. She no longer had to wonder where Pike was. She found him. She took a step back to peer behind a stone column to ensure that he or the blonde couldn't see that she was watching them. She didn't know how long she stayed hidden in the dark, but she was there long enough to see him and the mystery woman from his past sitting next to each other on a long sofa before the large heath that took up an entire wall. The two of them were talking and laughing. She lost count of the number of times that the woman touched him. The girl said something that caused him to lean back in mock surprise. Cashmere's eyes narrowed when the woman pulled on his arm. Not resisting, he leaned toward her. The woman laughed as she pushed the hair that had fallen into his face back before she kissed him on the cheek. Cashmere turned away to return back to the room, but not before their raised voices and laughter rung out again.

The next morning, Cashmere got up; still fire hot over what she had seen. The fact that his side of the bed seemed slept in did nothing to cool her anger. Today, she wasn't going to let him give her a smile and a few words as he passed by. He was going to tell her what the hell he was up to. Where the hell he gets off bring her all the way here, and then spend his nights with another chick? He wasn't going to lock her way in some godforsaken place while he played that, 'if I can't have you, no one can' game with her. She didn't ask him to step up. She had been happy doing things her own way.

She groaned at the pain that shot through her scalp at the force she brushed her hair. Wanting to make sure she kept her edges, she took her time pulling her straighten hair up on top of her head to fashion it into a messy bun. Stopping in the bathroom to wash her face and brush her teeth, she quickly pulled on a pair of jean shorts, a dark gray tank top, and the hiking boots he had bought for her. She doubted she would even feel the cool air; she was so worked up. She didn't care if it took her all day to track him down. Lucky for her, she didn't have to go far. All she had to do was follow the loud voices to the main hall. This time, she didn't hide behind a column on the landing.

"Is that her?"

Pike looked up to the left to see Cashmere marching across the landing overhead toward the stairs.

"Yeah, that's her," replied Demont, answering Shamus' question.

"I think that's a perfect storm coming your way," beamed Angus.

"Shit, more like a typhoon," laughed Demont, which caused a roar of laughter from the group of eight men that were standing around a large table.

Pike turned around just in time to greet Cashmere.

"Good morning. Let me introduce you to some of my family. This is-"

"Hi," she said with a wave, cutting him off. Her brown eyes never left his. "I need to talk to you," she stated as she took a step back.

He smiled and led the way across the main hall and around the corner. Demont waited until the pair was out of sight before he leapt to his feet to follow behind them with the other men in tow to listen in.

As soon as they had rounded the corner, Cashmere let him have it.

"I want to leave."

Pike stopped in his tracks and turned around. "Excuse me," he said with a grin. The blinding sun coming through the windows made his dark green sparkle.

"I want to go home. I'm done with this shit. First, you break into my room. Then you bring me here with all these promises, but you don't even deliver," she spat.

"If you want me to fuck you, all you need to do is ask," he chuckled.

Cashmere grinded her teeth as she clenched her fists. "Were you with her since I've been here?"

"Who?"

"Don't play fuckin coy with me," she fumed as she put her hands on her hips. "The chick you were swapping spit with in the pictures in your room."

Pike's eyebrow went up as his smile deepened. Demont had told him that she had been asking about him. The fact that she was jealous had a strange effect on him. It frustrated him that she would think that his desire for her would be that fickle. He wanted her, and no one else. It also excited him that she would be mad at the thought that he might be spending his time with another.

"Have you ever been diagnosed as bipolar?" he laughed as he shook his head.

She sized him up and down with her narrowed gaze. There he was in a pair of relaxed acid wash jeans that hung low enough on his hips that she was able to glimpse the ginger hair that ran down the front of his fit stomach to disappear into his pants. The red cotton T-shirt stretched over his muscular chest and arms to perfection. Once again, his hair was a mess and hung free.

"Where are you going?" she grunted.

"I can't stand here while you stare at me like you're crazy," he threw back over his shoulder as he traced his steps back to the main hall. He walked around the corner and crashed into the group of men that had been listening to them argue. He tossed back his head and laughed.

"I'm going with you," Cashmere announced.

Pike shrugged his shoulder as he kept walking toward the front door.

"We're just going to be riding out over the land to expect some herds, but we're going to be riding a lot today," he warned her.

She would be damned if she was going to be left behind. She walked next to him as he led the way to the stables. By the time that they had reached the large area, it was already abuzz with the men picking out their mounts.

"Just wait while I find you a horse," he commanded.

If she had thought that she would like being dominated by him in the bedroom, she hated taking commands from him outside of it.

"I'll just ride him," she remarked as she pointed at the chestnut beast of a horse she rode with him the other day.

Everyone in the stables watched the showdown between the two of them closely. To say they were amused would have been putting it lightly.

"That's not a good idea. I know you said you know how to ride, but not him," he replied as he took hold of her arm to stop her.

"Bullshit," she snapped, pulling her arm free. Without another word, she walked up to the horse, placed her foot in the stirrup and pulled herself up.

What happen next, no one could have kept from happening. The horse took off running out of the stables with all the men in hot pursuit. Luckily, he didn't go too far before he stopped and reared up on his hind legs. Cashmere tried to hold on, but she lost her grip. She fell back and landed in the large pile of manure that had been shoved out of the stables. Everyone was silent in pure shock before the roar of laughter rung out in the morning sun. The sight of her sitting up, slowly, completely covered in shit only made everyone laugh even harder.

"Are you alright?" laughed Pike as he ran to her side.

"I...I," she mumbled in fear of some getting in her mouth.

"I guess he sensed he had a bitch riding on his back," he laughed.

He took a big step back to make sure none got on him while she got to her feet.

"You guys go on ahead. I'll take her to the lake to clean up," he ordered. He gladly took the lye soap his cousin Shamus had fetched for him from the stables. "Follow me," he chuckled.

She wanted to cry as she walked wide leg and stiffly after him. It didn't take long for the flies that had been flying over the pile of shit to start encircling around her. It seemed as if it took forever to reach the large body of water. On the edge of the lake, she stepped out of her shoes.

"Get in," grunted Pike from behind her. Sucking his teeth, he shoved her forward and into the water. She fell like a stone, only to come up screaming.

"My hair!" she yelled.

"And my fuckin nose, woman!" he shouted.

That was the first time she heard it. His Irish accent sounded alluring to her ears.

"Now take off your clothes and toss them over here."

A chill ran down her spine. She wondered if it was due to the temperature of the water or the fact that he was stepping out of his high top sneakers to join her in the water. She took off her shorts first. Then her tank top and bra came off next. She was just waist deep, but then she walked further out until her breasts were immersed. She turned back to watch him undress. This was her first time seeing him naked, and she didn't want to miss it.

Pike tossed her clothes over by a large tree. He then reached behind his head and jerked off his shirt. Next, he unbuckled his belt and opened his jeans. They fell to the grass in a hush. Cashmere's greedy eyes feasted at the sight of his toned, fit body, his broad shoulders, his muscular arms, and his thick, long cock that was growing in size and length right before her eyes. He bent down, picked up the soap, and stepped in the water. If the coolness of it bothered him, it never registered on his handsome face. Step by step, his tempting body was swallowed up by the lake. That thought might have upset her, but each step brought him closer to her as well.

"Let me help you," he offered when he finally made it over to her. He reached up and pulled the headband she had used to secure her hair out. "I actually hate your hair straight," he admitted. "Lean back," he commanded.

His hand snaked around her waist. She let her feet float up. Pike stepped in between her legs and guided them around his waist as he balanced her. She leaned back into the water, letting her scalp get wet. Pike's eyes fastened on her breasts that floated above the water.

It was just too much for him to resist. He didn't care that she was still covered in shit in some places. He lowered his head, opened his mouth wide, and began to suckle on her right nipple. He brought his left hand around and cupped her other breast. He felt her body stiffen from the force of his suction. Her legs tightened around his waist to pull him closer. Slowly, he rose his head to glimpse her looking up at him. He lowered her back to her feet to tower over her five-foot-two self. Without a word, he soaped up his calloused hands. He washed her chest, her arms, then upward to her neck. He applied pressure on her shoulder to signal for her to lower herself into the water to remove the soap. Taking the soap again, he reached up and began to wash her head. He watched her as she closed her eyes to enjoy the sensation of him massaging her scalp.

Her eyes popped open at the sudden change in his grip. He pulled hard on her hair, forcing her head back. He leaned forward. Pike started at her throat as he licked the water clean off her skin to her chin, then to her bottom lip. She opened her mouth, and he inhaled her sigh as he covered her mouth with his. His kiss was slow while he held her head still to receive his kiss. Cashmere's hands moved to his collarbone. Her touch was light as her fingertips traced it. Downward, she continued her exploration of his body over his muscular chest, over his ribcage, his ripped abs, to his hip bones, and onward along the defined cut of his torso which took her hands under water.

Pike let out a deep moan at the feel of her hand gripping his hard cock. He smiled against her mouth when her hand went to the base then back up slowly to measure his length. She gasped when the revelation of his size and special quality registered in her mind.

"It's curved," she panted in awe, like a crescent moon. She hadn't noticed that when he had stripped. There was a slight curve in the middle of his dick that caused it to not be the normal straight ride. Even with the curvature, his dick still reached at least five inches above his belly button. He had the length and girth to reach and stretch her wide.

"For your pleasure," he teased as he nibbled on her bottom lip.

"I hope you'll feel the same way about me," she mumbled.

Pike lifted his head to glare down at her. She could read his confused expression.

"I might as well tell you. It only happened twice, but it was enough to make me worry about how you would react. I have incredibly strong muscles, and when I get extremely excited, they clap down...hard," she explained. Her heart dropped into her stomach when he took a step back to stare at her, blankly. His silence combined with the strange look on his face made all her fears come rushing back. There was no doubt in her mind that Pike would take her to a level of excitement that she had only experienced twice in her life when she was still learning her body, with only one man that was a very talented lover.

"Let's go," grunted Pike as he pushed her towards the grass.

"What? Wait, my hair," she screamed.

"Yeah, right." He had completely forgotten about the soap that was still in it. His mind was on other things after her revelation. Swiftly, he helped her clean her hair.

"Ok, time to get out."

"Where are we going?" she cried, fearfully.

Pike pulled her back into his arms. He ran his right hand over her taut stomach until he parted her legs. He lifted her leg with his left hand as he slipped his two fingers into her pussy. "I'm going to experience just what this pussy of yours can do," he moaned, hotly against her ear.

Cashmere's hand went under the water to guide his fingers deeper.

"More...deeper" she begged.

He watched her buck her hips as she created ripples in the water while she rode his fingers. He closed his eyes as the walls of her pussy contracted to hold his fingers in. She was tight as hell. If he hadn't known her background, he would have sworn that she was a virgin. He considered mounting her from behind just to get a preview of what was to come, but as his green eyes scanned the land around them, he quickly decided to wait. He knew that once he started, there would be no stopping. The thought of food or drink wouldn't matter. He was going to fuck his brains out once he got her back to his room.

"Cashmere, we only have to make it upstairs." They both grunted in protest as he withdrew his fingers. She didn't need any more coaxing. She practically ran to the shore.

"My clothes."

Pike turned and picked up his cotton T-shirt. That's when she saw it. He glared back at her thinking that something was wrong.

"Your back," she pointed. She took the shirt from his hand while she examined the massive tattoo that covered his entire back. The image of a wicked leprechaun with a top hat, sitting on a bag of gold paid homage to his Irish heritage. The mythical creature held a wooden pipe; he was smoking in one hand while he held a piece of shiny gold in the other. The fact that it was just a black outline with shading added to the eerie background of the forest, the night sky, and the demon faces that were hidden in the roots of the tree stump that acted as the back of the leprechaun's throne.

"I know it's a lot to absorb," he said, sheepishly while he stepped into his pants. He didn't even bother to fasten them.

"I think it's breathtaking. Whoever did it, did an awesome job," she whispered as she caressed his back. "It makes me wonder what other things you've been holding back from me? Ah, I see there's more," she chuckled when he turned around to face her, but he kept his eyes hidden from her.

Swiftly, he scooped up his shoes, grabbed her hand, and led the way around to the front of the castle. His hands itched to slid under the hem of the shirt she was wearing to fondle her naked flesh underneath. Everyone they passed looked at them with knowing eyes as they made their way up the stairs and into the home. He kept his hand on the small of her back while they walked. Both tried to pace their steps not to appear too eager, but all bets were off as soon as they crossed the landing that overlooked the main hall.

He grabbed her and threw her against the wall. His hands were everywhere, and she liked it. Cashmere grabbed his ass and pulled him closer. The feel of his hard dick pressing into her stomach made her light headed with desire. She shoved him away and started to speed walk down the maze of halls, and through the wooden door toward the winding stone steps that lead to his room. Pike bit his bottom lip. With each step she took up the stairs, his shirt that stopped just a few inches under her round ass, rose to gift him with a glimpse of her brown ass cheeks. He swore loudly. She let out a yell when he shoved her against the wall.

"Part your legs for me," he panted from behind her.

She could feel the softness of the mushroom shaped tip of his dick brushing her bare ass.

"Like this?" she teased. She slowly widened her legs. "Or would you prefer me like this?" She lifted her leg to rest against the wall like a bitch in heat.

Pike ran his hand over the inner thigh of her lifted leg until he reached her shaved pussy lip. He touched her clit, then ran his strong finger over her open, moist center. He rubbed her throbbing hole with the head of his cock. She reached back to urge him on. Pike took hold of her wrists in a vise-like grip and held them over her head.

"You'll feel me moving inside you in due time," he promised as he grabbed his dick at the root and began to wet his tip again with her pussy juices.

"When I get you in that room, I'm going to fuck you till you're raw," he moaned as he began to force the head of his cock into her willing body. "I'm going to pump you with so much cum that when you walk by every man will smell it on you...in you," he grunted.

Her scream echoed throughout the confined stairway due to the force of him penetrating her body. He withdrew to the tip of his dick, then feed his cock back into her pussy. He repeated that action a few more times to get her used to the feel of his cock. She was small compared to his six foot four muscular frame. He marveled at how wet she became with each of his strokes.

"Just a little bit more, and you'll have all of it," he moaned. Pike bent his knees and thrust forward, this time until he was buried deep.

"Oh God," she cried. "What are you doing? Don't fuckin stop now!" she shouted when he began to back away out of fear that he had hurt her.

That's all he needed to hear. He lowered his head and began to pound her against the wall. In no time, he began to feel what she had warned him about. It was unlike anything he had experienced. Just like with his fingers, her pussy was like a suction drawing him in while it got tighter with each stroke. Thankfully, it also got wetter and wetter as well, or he would have gotten chaff from all the friction.

"I need a bed. Hold on."

Swiftly, he let her hands go, pulled her back into a tight embrace with his strong arms supporting her weight and keeping her from falling forward. Cashmere brought her hands back and held on to his neck to steady herself while he took the stairs two at a time. With each step, his dick thrusted in her, keeping her on the verge of cumming. He stopped along the way up the stairs to kick off his falling pants. Completely nude, he walked into his room, kicked the door closed, and marched to the bed to position her face down. Without skipping a beat, he rose her hips and began to fuck the hell out of her. His strong hands cut into her hips as he began to lift her knees from the bed.

Cashmere clawed the bed, only for him to pull her back to meet his powerful thrusts. She felt as if he was penetrating through her stomach and into her chest; he was so deep. He paused as he rotated his hips to stretch her flesh even wider.

Pike glanced down to watch his dick reappear from the depths of her body. He licked his lips at the creamy nectar that covered his cock. He ran his finger down his length then licked his finger. One taste wasn't enough. Quickly he withdrew completely. Dropping to his knees, he licked her pussy from her swollen clit to her pink hole.

"So damn sweet," he said before he stabbed her cunt with his tongue, repeatedly. He commanded her to roll over onto her back. The look in his emerald green eyes was intense as he opened her legs wide.

"My God, you are so fuckin sexy, Cashmere. Every damn thing about you makes me want to love you," he confessed. He got back down to his knees, spread her pussy lips with his fingers before he began to lap at her pink center. He took his time sucking, stabbing, humming, and flicking her clit. She laced her fingers in his head to hold him in place as he sucked on her clit.

"Fuck Pike," she whimpered as she rotated her hips.

"Yes," he teased, as he wiped her juices from his face.

"No, I want to cum," she grumbled when he got to his feet.

"And you will," he chuckled while he positioned himself between her shaking legs. She gasped and moaned as he pushed into her body. He watched her every expression on her brown face. He wanted to commit it all to memory. "Hold on."

She reached down, grabbed his ass, and push him forward as she raised her hips to meet him. His kiss matched the rhythm of his hips. In and out, he pounded her with no mercy. Slipping his arm under her leg, he maneuvered it to rest on his shoulder as he grinded his hips in an attempt to make a closer, deeper connection.

"Damn it," he groaned. Her sharp nails dug into his back.

"Let's see who'll bleed first."

Pike narrowed his eyes.

"You make me want to-"

"Do it," she challenged.

Pike went still of a second. A wicked grin spread across his handsome face. This time, when he started, there was no holding back. He dominated her like no other lover in her past had. He bucked his hips with speed and deepness that had her crying out. With a mixture of long and short, deep and shallow strokes, he owned her body. He rested his sweaty head on the mattress as he continued his assault.

"Oh Lord," she moaned when his teeth bit her neck before he sucked hard on her flesh. She was sure there would be marks on her neck and shoulders later. His actions only served to take her even higher.

He felt the first hard tremble of her pussy walls. It was definitely harder than anything he had experienced with any previous lover. He whispered hotly in her ear how her body felt and how it was making his dick feel in great detail.

"I can feel it. Dear Lord, you feel like heaven. Shit, you got my dick so wet, but I know I can make this pussy wetter."

He arched his back and began to put the curvature of his cock to good use by tapping on that spot in her pussy that he was sure was going to make it rain. He already felt his dick getting slicker and slicker with each penetrating thrust.

"Fuck," he said in a guttural voice. He leaned up to gaze down upon Cashmere in complete awe. Her orgasm was so strong that he couldn't move at all. The walls of her cunt had clamped down so hard that his dick was trapped. With each wave, that coursed through her body, his cock was massaged with each hard tremor of her cunt. He bit down on his lip and closed his eyes while he both enjoyed the outer body, sensual experience, her body was gifting him and tried not to cum in the process.

Cashmere was blinded and left with no senses. It was as if all the blood had been routed to that one spot in her body. Her entire body felt as if it had gone up in flames. Fucking Pike was all she had imagined and more.

There's no way you can walk away from him, the voice in her mind sang.

"Is it like that every time?" panted Pike with a handsome smile on his face.

"That all depends on you," she teased, now back on Earth.

"Well, let's see what I can do," he chuckled before he began to move, slowly.

Five hours later, a very sore and sweat drenched Cashmere hobbled into the bathroom. Every muscle in her body ached; even her teeth from grinding them, her throat from screaming, and her toes from curling them. This was the only place Pike hadn't had sex with her. He had worked his way through the room as he tested out the walls, the leather chairs, the floor, up against the window, bent over the footboard, and every spot on the bed, in positions that had to have come out of a book. She was sure that if she left for home today, she was full with enough of his cum to have his baby. He was like a beast that just kept going. Her body shined from the sweat on her mocha colored skin. She smiled as she looked at the tiny bite marks and hickeys he left on her on her breasts, shoulders, her neck, her stomach, and when she looked lower, on her upper inner thighs very close to her pussy. She felt her heart flip in her chest when she caught sight of the stream of watery white liquid that stained the inside of her leg.

She leaned on the sink and pushed her damp, curly hair from out of her face. She frowned for a second while she regarded her long locs that cascaded past her shoulders. She never really liked having so much hair, but she had it for as long as she could remember. Her mother always said that men liked a woman with long hair. She longed to cut it or maybe even color it, but her mother's words always stopped her. Even now as an adult, with some sense of position, the teachings of her mother had so much to do with every decision she had ever made, and her desire to make that woman proud.

She closed her eyes. Already she felt the tug -of-war between her duty and her heart. The line had been crossed. He had taken her into his world and his bed. The reaction of being with him was a hundred times stronger than what she had thought it would be. They had been friends for so long as it was. Now with this newfound closeness, she already felt herself falling for the handsome man she had been secretly digging on. She could feel the warmth from his body long before his hot hand caressed her spine.

"Are you going to make it, Peaches?"

"Yes."

"Tell me what's wrong?" he ordered as he snaked his strong arms around her. His eyes scanned her face through the reflection in the mirror.

"Do you think I would look good with short hair? Not too short, but shorter?"

Pike blinked a few times from her question. He had thought something really important had been on her mind because of the expression that had been on her face when he entered the bathroom.

"My question to you is, would *you* like it shorter?" He watched her feelings play out across her face. He narrowed his eyes while he waited. It shocked him for a moment because he had seen that look before many times on someone else in his life.

"I don't kno-"

"Don't tell me you don't know?" he grumbled.

Her eyes found his in the mirror.

"You already know what you want. There isn't a right or a wrong answer, Cashmere. My feelings for you won't change if you were bald. Whatever makes you happy, makes me happy. End of story."

Chapter Six

The smile she gave him was blinding. In spite of it, he was seeing a part of her that he never knew existed. She appeared to be in such control on Ginger Island, but he glimpsed an uncertainty in her that many men would try to exploit for their own gain. He cautioned himself on the way he handled her from here on out. It drove him wild beyond what words could explain to dominate her in the bedroom, but he had no desire to control her in any other way. He wanted her to be a free thinker and not give two shits about what others would or wouldn't like. Just as long as they were happy, who gives a fuck about the outsiders. It would drive him crazy if she turned into a version of his own Mother.

"If you're done being vain, come back to bed," he teased as he smacked her hard on her ass, causing her to let out a loud yelp.

She made a big show of rubbing her stinging cheek as she walked slowly back into the bedroom. The aroma of food surprised her, due to the fact, that she hadn't heard him leave or return. Greedily, she got back into bed and began to eat the fried chicken he had piled on the plate along with some strawberries and grapes.

"Tell me about this new hairdo," he said while he positioned a few pillows behind him.

It was like old times. They picked right up from where their friendship had been. He had wonder how it would be between the two of them after they had become intimate. Unlike so many friendships that had been ruined, when it was taken out of the 'friend zone', there was no strangeness in their communication. They laughed and teased each other like always. Even still, he did notice a slight change. There was a tenderness in the way she teased him. The way she would give him a heated look that was full of desire, or how she would focus on his mouth when he spoke; only for her to look away, sheepishly when she caught herself staring. Also, how she used any excuse to touch him. He did his best not to glance down at her pussy that was exposed to him in the Indian style way she had chosen to sit on the bed before him, but he knew she saw his green gaze slip once or twice.

"I didn't hurt you, did I?" Questioned Pike as he touched a purpled hickey on her breast.

Her body responded immediately to the sound of his deep voice and touch. She hid her brown eyes behind her lazy lids. She swallowed hard.

"No," she answered, a bit breathless.

"Forgive me for asking... and I don't want to offend you in any way, but did you *enjoy* being with me? I mean, all of this?" he whispered.

She closed her eyes as his began to touch the marks he had left on her mocha skin.

"Fuck Pike, don't do that to me," she remarked in a thick tone.

He touched the mark he left on her stomach softly.

"Why? What am I doing?" he inquired in a husky voice as if he didn't know.

She opened her eyes, "I enjoyed every damn thing you did to me, and no, I'm not reading from a script. I'm sure you made many women happy in this room."

"You are the *only* woman I made happy in this room. I would never disrespect this house by bringing a cheap lay here."

"Not even Blondie?"

"She hasn't had the pleasure, nor will she ever. I know what you've said, but I'm *never* going to let you go back Cashmere. After I'm done with you, you won't want to," he promised.

He reached out and drug her against him before she was able to respond. Unknowing to him, she didn't have anything to say. His words had touched her so deeply, that she was rendered completely speechless.

"Don't mind him," he chuckled as he moved his stiffening cock to the side so she could lay down on top his body. "Get some sleep."

Cashmere placed her head on his chest and relaxed. It only took her a short while of listening to his strong heartbeat before she felt her eyes close and she was fast asleep. Pike let his head fall back on the headboard. His mind was filled with questions and doubts, but being the man that he was, he quieted every voice that spoke against what he wanted. There was no way he was going to lose this woman. He was willing to move Heaven and Earth and wrestle an angel; if that's what it took. Cashmere was going to be his.

***

As the week went on, she fell further down the rabbit hole. She no longer had to wonder about where Pike was because he was with her every night. They had created a routine with their days. They would wake up each morning and enjoy having lazy sex. He always took his time with her as the early morning sun shone upon them. Then he would start a bath for her only to return with breakfast before he joined her in the large wooden tub. Later, he would go to the small office in the other room to take care business while she explored the many rooms of the castle.

She was happy for those times alone to think. In two weeks, her period was due to come on, making her total time with him three weeks. When she missed it, which she was sure it wouldn't be coming on, there was no need for her to stay. She would be with child. She bit her lip as the thought of having his baby excited her, but what that would mean, also made her heart ache. She had stopped correcting him whenever he spoke of her staying with him. In his mind, they were building a family, but she knew otherwise.

She gazed out the window as her mind took her back to yesterday. Pike found her in the library late in the afternoon. He looked handsome in the gray sweat pants and a tank top that clung to his muscular chest. He hadn't shaved since they had arrived, but she didn't mind. In fact, she found his beard to be very sexy.

"Come with me," he had ordered.

Cashmere took his outstretched hand. He didn't say a word as he guided her through the maze of his home to a wing that she hadn't explored. He lifted the heavy iron latch and opened the door. Confused, she walked into the large empty room that hadn't been done to match the rest of the updated parts of the castle. He stood silently with his hands behind his back, but his eyes followed her as she explored the large room and the adjacent room next door.

"I was thinking that this would become our room and the one through there would be the nursery for the baby," he explained. He took note of the expression that crossed her face before she composed herself. It had been excitement.

"Pike, you need to stop this shit," she tried to say in an angry tone, but it came up short.

"You'll have to decide on the renovations, but I'm here to help you if you need it," he continued as if she hadn't said anything at all. Without another word, he had turned and left her there.

She wasn't surprised to find herself standing in front of the door now. Since that conversation, that room was all she could think of. She opened the door and came face to face with Demont and a few of Pike's cousins.

"I didn't expect anyone to be here," she said, sheepishly.

"Well, the boy is excited about getting started on the room, although, I told him not to get the cart before the horse," winked Demont.

"He might already have the horse with all the work he's been putting into it," joked Shamus.

Cashmere rolled her eyes as she walked further into the room.

"So, what are your thoughts...about the rooms?" asked Demont.

"I wouldn't worry about the baby's room," she answered.

Demont regarded her strangely due to her response. He told the other men to take a break. He waited into they cleared the room before he spoke. He wasn't going to dance around the bush. He was never that kind of man.

"What the fuck are you doing, girl?"

Cashmere took a step back in shock.

"Excuse me?"

"No, I won't be, excusing you. Don't tell me you haven't returned the boy's affections. Are you fuckin daft, or something? This man is willing to take you as you are, and you're going back to that place," he remarked in awe.

"You need to stay out of my business."

"Shit, if you're pregnant, it is my business. We're family," he grunted. "Why would you even want to go back to that place to be passed around, any damn way?"

"I'm not passed around," she pointed out as she squared her shoulders.

"Oh, pardon me, your highness," he bowed, mockingly.

Silence fell over the room as she considered her answer.

"It is stupid of me to go back, isn't it? I mean, what woman that has a choice would choose to be a whore. Pike never cared about what I was, and he still doesn't. Why the fuck should I go back? Shit, I'm twenty-seven years old...and do I want to bring my child up in a brothel when it could have all of this?" she finished with a wave of her hand.

Demont felt she was talking more to herself than him, but he still amen'd everything she said.

"I heard many myths about this place," she started as she strolled over to the window to look out. "You know a story is a myth because it's just too good to be true, or the things that happen just don't happen to real people. My mother never told me stories because she said it was a waste of time...that I needed to be logical; that shit like that is what would keep me from having what was rightfully mine."

"Sorry if this hurts you, Lass...but your Mom sounds like a real asshole. Why should you give up your *one* life to do what another says?"

"I don't know anything else. What other skill do I have? I can barely read," she cried.

"But I've seen you with books in the library," he whispered in shock.

"I'm looking at the pictures. My math skills are fantastic, and I watch the news and documentaries for facts, but my Mom didn't allow me to be educated. I know how to navigate in that world, but out here...on my own," she shook her head.

Demont examined the girl with new eyes. He hated himself for attacking her the way he just did. If her mother was there, he would have beaten the damn woman for what she had done to her daughter to ensure she had a life of servitude. He had heard some fucked up things in his life, but this took the cake. Now he could understand her fear of *not* going back to the only place she knew. She would be taking a big risk on Pike not to grow tired of her like many men do.

"You know what's so funny?" she sighed, painfully. "Since I took the reins of that place, I've made it so the women there could get a college degree in whatever they want, so they'll have a choice. Meanwhile, I'm the dumbest one out of the bunch; that's stuck there."

"Many men don't give a damn about having a smart woman."

"Oh, you're right about that. If she can fuck and suck, then she's a keeper, and I've been trained by the best...but what happens to those women when it gets old? When that man want's more, or something shiny and new? Or when I do something that embarrasses Pike because I can't read the fuckin headline on the got damn newspaper. I know his brother. Shit, I know his Dad. There is no hiding what I am."

His heart jerked when she glanced at him, and he saw her wet, red eyes. She had been looking away from him before to hid the fact that she was crying. He cleared the lump that had formed in his throat, "Have I told you about that lake down there?" he asked softly. "They say that at night, the fairies light it up when they come to the lake to bathe. They say that if you're there to see it, and you dip yourself in the water, your wish will be granted."

"They're just fireflies," she smirked.

"Why you got to ruin it for me, Lass?" groaned Demont.

Pike heard Cashmere's laughter echo all the way into the hall. He had come to see what was going on after his cousins had sent him a text to tell him that she and Demont were having it out. He had run all the way there, and he as happy he had. He wouldn't have never known her secret, if he hadn't. He had just assumed that she had been educated, but now that he thought about it, she had never read before him. Now, those moments of uncertainty, that he had seen in her since coming here took on a whole new meaning.

He remained in the hallway with his forehead pressed against the wall as he listened to them tease each other for another ten minutes before he broke up the party. He strolled into the room in his bare feet as if he didn't know a thing. Even though his face hid his true feelings, his heart ached to embrace her. He wanted her to reveal her secret to him, so he could assure her that he didn't care about it. Hell, he would even teach her without anyone knowing so that she didn't have to be frightened or ashamed. All this time he had thought that she was running away from *him*, but now he knew it was shame, fear, and a scene of duty that was making it hard for her to give in; which he knew she really wanted to do.

He walked behind her, pulled her hair back, and kissed a fading mark on her neck. His green eyes met Demont's. The man could see the anger flash in their depths. He wondered if the boy was upset with him, but he knew to wait till they were alone to question the lad.

"You couldn't stay away," he whispered as he touched her stomach, briefly before he stepped back.

"It isn't every day that a woman is given a reason to decorate," she teased.

"So, you have been thinking about it," smiled Pike. He held up his hand to stop her from ruining the moment. "Just humor me, please...if this was your home, what would you do to this room?"

Cashmere shrugged her shoulder as if to say, 'What the hell.'

Both men stood back as the floodgates of the creativity took center stage. She talked about colors, furniture, flooring, removing walls to add a large bathroom and two master closets. As for the nursery, she talked about storage, but nothing else. She couldn't bring herself to indulge in that fantasy even for one second. Pike listened to her suggestions. He asked questions whenever he was confused by her decisions until he completely had her vision.

"That's a major undertaking," grunted Demont.

"Well it's just a thought, that's why it will probably won't become a reality," she said, slowly.

Demont's gaze darted over to Pike. He saw him clenching his teeth while he glared at the girl with narrowed eyes.

"Has that other issue been taken care of?" inquired Pike as he switched the topic.

"No, they're still running wild, but I warned you that you need to take care of that from day one," answered Demont.

Pike ran his fingers through his hair. Suddenly he felt tired. Why did it seem as if fate was betting against him, he wondered?

"We'll take care of it before they get too out of hand," he promised. He left the room without even saying good-bye to her.

The rest of the day, he kept himself busy while he tried to figure out how to scale the wall that had been presented to him. It was much later when he entered their room. She was surprised to see that he was dripping wet. She wondered if he gotten caught in a storm, but then she noticed his unopened pants. The image of the mystery blonde sprung to mind before she crushed it down. She turned down the smooth jazz she had been listening to while she waited for him to come to bed. They had never skipped a night of sex, so she had been eagerly awaiting him.

"Where were you?"

"I took a bath in the lake,"

"Praying to the fairies?" she teased.

Pike smirked as he kept his gaze from her, "And if I was, would you laugh?"

She frowned when he didn't come to bed, but instead, he took a seat before the blazing fire. Cashmere watched him as he got lost in the dancing flames. Slowly, she slipped from the bed to stand in front of him.

Pike looked up at her from his slumped sitting position. He feasted on her body in the sheer cream colored nightgown she was wearing; if that's what you would call it. There was nothing hidden from his heated gaze. His breath caught in his throat as she began to lower herself between his legs. His eyes were trained on her slender fingers as they unzipped his jeans to release his throbbing cock. He bit his bottom lip hard at the first contact of her full, soft lips brushing against the mushroom shaped tip of his head. Her hands held his dick at the root, firmly for her opened mouth.

"Heaven help me," he prayed as his cock disappeared inch by inch into her hot, moist mouth. In spite of his size, she was able to deep throat his entire length. His hands cupped the back of her head while he guided her down until her lips touched his curly pubic hair. He held her there until he felt her body jerk as she began to gag on his cock.

"Shit," he groaned at the feel of her throat contracting before she withdrew enough of his length, sending a wave of saliva cascading down his dick to moisten his nuts. The slurping sounds she made with her mouth as she began to suck his dick in earnest, made his eyes roll back in his head. He gripped her hair and began to fuck her mouth. She relaxed her jaws and created a willing hole for him to thrust into repeatedly. Suddenly, he stopped. He pulled her onto his chest.

"We have to slow down," he panted. He took a steadying breath and kissed her. He took his time as he slowly played with her tongue.

Finaly, he broke away. He ran his thumb over her mouth while his green eyes bore into her brown ones. He tilted his head.

"I want you to do something for me. I don't care if you have to pretend, just let me believe in the fantasy," he said in a deep voice that causes the butterflies in her stomach to take flight.

She nodded her head.

"I want you to make love to me," he whispered. Pike saw the shock register in her eyes before she closed them.

The raw, pure emotion in his words rocked her to the core. When she opened her eyes, they were moist with tears because she knew then what she had been afraid to admit to herself. She was in love with this man. His request was an easy one because she had felt that way for so long. She got to her feet. Slowly, her shaking hand went to the straps of her nightgown. Pike watched at it fell to the floor. She stepped back between his legs. He sat up and began to caress her body gently with his fingertips. Her hard nipples, her breasts, down her breastbone, over her rib cage, to her stomach; which is where he paused for a moment before he went to the apex of her thighs. He slid his two fingers into the gap between her thighs to brush against her shaved pussy. It dampened the top of his fingers with her nectar. Cashmere opened her legs enough for him to insert his two fingers into her body. Pike gazed up to watch the firelight illuminate her expressions of pleasure on her brown face as his fingers glided inside her. With his free hand, he shoved his jeans down his legs and kicked them off. He guided her closer as he leaned back in the leather chair.

Cashmere reached down and removed his hand. She stopped him from licking his fingers clean. Instead, she brought his glistening fingers to her own mouth to suck her juices from them, before she straddled his legs. Reaching down, she held his bucking dick in hand as she impaled herself onto his engorged flesh until he was firmly seated inside her. They both moaned from the pleasure of being joined as one. She rotated her hips, drawing him in deeper before she began to ride him slowly. Pike rested his hands on her hips as he let her have her way.

She leaned forward and rested her head in the crook of his neck. He whispered tender words of affection in her ear as she bounced up and down. It didn't take long for her to realize this wasn't like the other times. This was real. Pike genuinely loved her. The revelation shocked her, causing her to stiffen her body.

"Please, Cashmere...don't stop now," he begged. He pushed her back to look at her. He touched her face, tenderly. "Don't mess it up. Make me feel like you love me," he panted. The tears on her cheeks sparkled in the light. "Are you crying for me because I'm silly to dream, or because you love me, too?" he whispered as he wiped her cheeks.

He watched her from under hooded lids while she continued to make love to him. Even though he longed to hear her say that she loved him too, he knew that she did. The way she touched him, gazed down at him, kissed him, he knew.

But will she stay? He pondered as he remained still until her pussy loosened enough to allow him to move freely again. When he did, he kept the same tender, slow tempo she had set until he released his hot seed into her body, yet again.

Chapter Seven

Neither one spoke of that night. Pike didn't want to press her anymore. While Cashmere just wanted to enjoy the time they had left together. With two weeks down, and now two days into the third, she was a hot mess of emotions. Even more so now that he had brought up the subject of getting a test to see if she was with child or not. Quickly, she had shot down the idea. She knew from the telling look in his green eyes that he knew why she didn't want to cause the time they had left to be gone in the matter of a blue line on a damn stick.

"You'll have to take one sooner or later," he smiled with a shrug. He then went on to guess how their child would look. Thinking about it now made her heart contract in within her chest.

Even if you leave him, you won't be able to go back to the way you were. Then again, he just won't let your ass leave, the voice in her mind pointed out as she got dressed for the day.

There was a big part of her that like the idea of him putting his foot down and forcing her to stay with him in this castle. Then she could bitch and moan; all the while she was happy to be with him.

But how would that be fair to him? No one wants to strong arm another into loving them. He deserves all of you and to know you've given it.

"I'm driving myself crazy," she mumbled under her breath as she walked out the door with her purse in hand.

She had to know. Cashmere marched down the stairs quickly. She sent up a silent prayer that Pike was off doing something so he wouldn't know she was leaving to go to the town that was only a short distance away. It wasn't her first time driving there. She scanned the great hall while she strolled across the landing. She just had to make it to the kitchen which is where he kept the keys to the *Rover*. She felt her stomach drop to her knees at the sound of male voices in the kitchen. Everyone turned at the loud noise of her sigh of relief; when she found it was only his two cousins Shamus and Angus standing by the sink.

"What the hell are you up to?" Questioned Angus while he eyed her carefully.

"I'm just running to town," she informed them, grabbing the keys off of the peg by the back door. She hesitated at the look the two exchanged, but decided not to worry about it on the account that she needed to go before anyone came in.

"Wait...we'll go with you!" yelled Angus, hot on her heels.

"Why? I've gone by myself before."

"We know that, but we just don't want nothing to happen to you, that's all," replied Shamus.

With a shrug, she accepted their answer. Logic told her that it was smart to have them with her. She was just a visitor. She didn't know anything about the people in that town, and the fact that she had tried to sneak out without telling anyone was a dumb one.

"Fine, you drive," she said, tossing the keys to Shamus.

The man smiled brightly, flashing Cashmere a dimple and the silver tooth in the front of his mouth. She hopped in the passenger side and strapped herself in for one hell of a ride. It seemed as if no one knew the concept of breaks in that part of the world. A trip that shouldn't have taken thirty minutes was done in sixteen.

"Where to?" he inquired.

"To the pharmacy."

They both stared at her with a wicked smile. It was no secret that they were trying for a baby. Pike made it very clear to the entire family that he was going to marry Cashmere, and if any of them opposed her, because of her race, then they better either pray to God for a better understanding or keep it to themselves. If anyone didn't like it, they hadn't let on. As for the two of them, they had grown to like the short, attractive woman and were considering casting their hats in the ring of finding themselves their own spot of chocolate.

"Don't say a word," she warned as she got out of the car to go in the store to buy a test. She wasn't put off by the stares she got when she walked in the store. To her knowledge, she was the only black person in the area. Even with that said, she was happy that Shamus and Angus had come along with her for the ride. The store was packed with people, and a few of the men were sneering as she walked down the aisles to the parent planning area. Her fears only multiplied when she went to the register to pay. Out of the corner of her eye, she saw a group of six men following her.

Not waiting to encourage them, she smiled and kept eye contact with the young girl behind the counter.

"So this here is the black bitch I've been hearing so much about," one of the men jeered in a heavy Irish accent.

"I so sorry," the red-headed girl whispered as she bruised herself to ring her up quickly.

"What's this?" said the man, snatching up the test from off the counter.

"The bitch is in heat," he said loudly, causing the other customers to look in their direction.

"The fuckin nerve of that asshole to disgrace the Irish blood by mixing it with a damn monkey," he spat, tossing the package back on the counter.

"Yeah, it should be *our* sister having his baby, not some black bitch," another man added as he took a step closer to her.

"He must be daft in the head. Don't he know he supposed to pull out of the blackies," the first man said, pushing Cashmere.

Quickly, she turned and made a beeline for the door.

"Hold up!" the man yelled as he and the other men fell in step behind her.

The front door seemed so far away as she began to run toward it. She didn't care about the products she knocked down in her frantic run. She could hear some of the other people shout to the men to stop and leave her alone, but they continued to chase her.

"Look at that ass jump. Shit, I want some of that," she heard too close for comfort behind her.

She paused at the door, due to the fact, that she forgot that she had to pull instead of push to make it out to the streets. She had just crossed the threshold when she felt a hand pull her roughly back. Cashmere let out a loud scream as she wheeled around to punch the man that had captured her. In a blink of an eye, the group had surrounded her on the street. They laughed down at her for her weak efforts to get free from them. Suddenly, Angus was there, fighting his way into the circle to pull her out of the men's grasp.

"Get in the car," he growled as he swung, catching one of the men in the jaw.

Cashmere clawed at the door, opened it, and locked the door.

"Are you alright?"

She was too shaken up to answer at that moment to answer Shamus.

"Drive!" commanded Angus as he hopped into the backseat.

She sat in the *Rover* as she listened to the two men curse all the way back to the house. She figured that someone must have texted Pike because he was running down the stairs completely dressed into the great hall by the time they busted through the front door.

"What the fuck happened?" growled Pike. He listened closely as the two retold the story of how they stopped the attack on Cashmere. He was like a statue while he gazed down upon a clearly shaken Cashmere. Silence fell over the great hall as he just stared until he finally spoke.

"Call it."

He had spoken the words so calmly, that she doubted he had spoken at all, but the other men heard it and understood what the phrase meant. Demont walked over and said something under his breath to Pike.

"I'm going to kill the mother fuckers. The whole fuckin family," he hissed. His Irish accent was back in full swing. His entire muscular frame shook with the rage that was coursing through him.

"Pike...Pike, wait," begged Cashmere, finding her tongue at last. "I'm fine. I..." she began as she walked to stand in front of him.

Pike took hold of her shoulders. She let out a groan at the amount of pressure he gripped her. He leaned down until their noses touched.

"I'm going to kill them," he repeated slowly, pronouncing each word before he pushed her away and walked out the door.

She turned to follow him only to be stopped by Demont.

"There's no use, Lass. It's been a long time coming. I'll do my best to keep him from killing them, though," he promised.

"Wait! I'm coming, too," Cashmere announced.

Demont stopped in his track. "It's going to be bloody," he warned.

"Can we hurry, please?"

"Ok," he sighed.

Her leg wouldn't stop bouncing on the drive to their destination.

"Maybe, we should call the police," she suggested.

"Oh, they'll be there, but not to stop it. Things are different here than in the States."

Forty minutes later, they pulled up to an abandoned building out in the middle of a field. People darted in front of Demont's truck while others ran down the lane toward the building. She hadn't expected to see such a large crowd.

"What the hell is going on?" she whispered, fearfully.

"They're all here for the same thing; to see Pike fight. He and Brick are a bit of a legend. Shit, there was a time that me and their Dad cracked skulls," he answered, matter of factly.

"Fight."

"Aye, girl. This once was a slaughterhouse, but now it's where we have our fight club."

"Oh, shit," she sighed, getting out of the car.

Even at their distance, they could hear the roar of the crowd coming from out of the wooden building. It was standing room only. It looked more like a scene from a *Mad Max* movie. Her eyes glanced upward to see that people were jammed in on the upper level to get a good view of the large ring that was in the middle of the room. Demont grabbed her hand to keep from getting separated from her as he pushed his way through the crush of people to get a good view of the ring.

Pike was already in the ring. He was yelling something to the men that were in there with him. She wished the crowd would shut the hell up so she could hear. She could barely see in the dim lit, smoky place. Suddenly, Angus was at her side.

"He's crazy. He's going to fight all three of those assholes!" he yelled over the screaming voices.

"What, wait! Do something," she demanded.

"Don't you think I tried," he answered.

"Before or after you placed our bet?" asked Demont.

"After," Angus winked.

Cashmere's eyes darted between the two of them as if they had lost their minds. She glanced back at the ring. She recognized the two stocky men from the store, but the other much older man, she hadn't seen before. The man looked like a thick ass ox. He was tall with arms that looked more like they had been chiseled out of stone.

"Just shoot their asses."

It was the men's turn to look at her as if she had lost her mind.

Demont opened his mouth to speak, but the activity in the ring commanded their attention. Pike reached over his head and removed his T-shirt.

"Oh shit," yelled Angus at the sight of his cousin's back tattoo that caused everyone in the room to shout. He had seen it a million times in this same ring, but it still had the same effect on him and the others that had seen him fight before. He had no doubt that Pike was going to fuck those assholes up. Even more so now that he had extra motivation to do so. Pike had speed, a hard head, brick-like fists and he had something that the three men in the ring didn't have; brains. He was able to pace himself.

"Listen," said Angus. "If you want him not to get hurt, just stay out of the way. You don't want to break his momentum because he sees you," he warned as he pulled her back between him and Demont.

Cashmere wasn't able to reply. In a blink of an eye, Pike's fist hit the man; that had so much to say in the store, in the mouth. The ref had to jump out of the way to keep from getting hit. The man stumbled back from the force of the hit. Quickly, he was pushed back towards Pike by his friends. Pike was waiting as he began to beat the hell out of his face. The man wasn't able to even get a hit in. Even as he fell to the ground, Pike followed him with his fist. She couldn't even see the man's face after the fifth hit, due to the blood that was covering it.

The second man from the store joined the fight. He punched Pike in the side of the head hard. She screamed at the sight of blood streaming from Pike's mouth. He stumbled back as the man rain down hits on Pike's head until he got it together. Pike charged the man, grabbing him at the waist. He kept his head down while he pushed the man backward, tripping him as he placed a few jabs at his ribs. Pike timed it just right. He let go of the man, letting gravity doing its job. He connected with the man's chin. He fell to his ass only for Pike to kick him hard in the face. Even over the crowd, she heard the cracking of the man's jaw.

Pike kicked him in his side a few times before he backed away. He wasn't going to make the same mistake he had done with the first man by being so focused on stomping him into the ground, that he took his eyes off of number three. He took a beating from the older man at the beginning of the fight because the man kept his face guarded. Pike's eye was now swollen, bruises on his side and blood was streaming from his lips and eye.

"What is he doing?" Cried Cashmere as she pulled at her hair.

"He's tiring him out!" shouted Angus. "Come on, Pike. Stop fuckin with him and finish it!" he yelled.

Pike shrugged as if he decided upon a plan of action. He took a step back. Instead of taking a swing, he kicked the old man in his knee. The man howled in pain, dropping his hands which left his face open. Once again, Pike chose to do the complete opposite of what she thought he would have done. He punched the man in his neck. Then as he dropped his head and grasped his throat. Pike grabbed his head, shoving it down to meet his knee as he brought it up hard. Blood from the man's nose and mouth stained Pike's jeans.

Pike limped back as the man fell like a stone to the ground. The ring was rushed by onlookers that wanted to touch Pike. Angus and Shamus ran to the ring to help Pike out. Cashmere wobbled on her legs with relief. She felt all her energy leave her body as if she had been the one throwing knees and elbows. She wanted to run to his side, but there were so many people surrounding him that she was in fear of being trampled. Again, Demont led her out of the building and back into the blinding light of the sun.

"Do you need a second?" inquired Demont as he rubbed her back.

She nodded her head. Her body shook with the adrenaline that coursed through her veins. She leaned on Demont while they walked to the car. On the way back to the home, she remembered something.

"That wasn't all about me, was it?"

Demont didn't need her to explain her question. "Actually, it was," he replied.

"But in the town, those guys said something about their sister."

Demont stole a glance at her. "That might be what *they* were fighting about, but *Pike* was fighting for an entirely different reason," he promised her.

The truck was still in motion when she ran out upon reaching the gravel driveway.

"Stop! Stop!" Yelled Demont as he jumped out of the running vehicle. "Give the doctor time to look him over and for him to get cleaned up, please."

Cashmere gulped down the lump in her throat. Maybe he was right.

"You better tell them to hurry cause I'm not waiting forever."

***

She leaned on the wall a few feet from the room door. She had originally been right outside the door so she could listen to his deep voice that carried through the thick wood door, but after she heard him laughing, she knew it looked worse than what it actually was. Thankfully, Shamus stayed with her to make the time pass until she was told she could enter. Her feet were heavy as she walked into the room. Her eyes sought him out. She found him propped up in the bed.

A grimace creased her face as she came closer. He looked like he had been an extra in the *Rocky* movie. His left eye was blue and purple. His right jaw was swollen as well as his lip. Her gaze went to the bandage that was wiped tightly around his ribs. Then, to his hands that were bruised and cut from pounding away on those men.

"Damn, Pike," she groaned, taking a seat next to him on the bed.

He rolled his eyes, "It looks worse than what it really is. No, I take that back. My ribs hurt like a muther fucker," he moaned.

"Then you shouldn't have fought over a damn girl, then. They would have gotten over you not getting with their sister, or whatever. What are you a fuckin kid!" she snapped, getting to her feet.

He pinned her with his narrow gaze as he leaned forward in the bed, "Ye must have maggots for brains. Those fuckin boggers can choke on my clackers. I don't give a rats arse about their box munching sister," he sneered, painfully in full Irish accent.

"Calm down, Pike," she ordered, backing away from the bed.

He tossed back the sheets, revealing his naked body underneath. "Come here," he shouted.

"No,"

"Get your arse over here, now or I'll come to you," he thundered.

She jumped at the sound of his voice. A chill rained down her spine as she tried to decide to obey him or not. She scanned the bruises on his body. If he tried to do anything, she would just punch him hard and run away. She bit her lip when she came to stand before him. The speed his hands moved to grab her, surprised her. First, she was on her feet. Then she was lying face down across his lap. He twirled his hand in her hair to keep her in place. This wasn't the first time he had put her in this position. She closed her eyes to await the touch of his hand on her ass.

Pike cursed under his breath as he pushed her off his lap. Quickly, he reached down, gripped her arms, and drug her to her knees. His mouth was crushing as he kissed her passionately. His hand pulled on her hair as he forced her head back. She was sure that his lips and face had to be in pain, but it didn't cause him to temper the force of his kiss.

He rested his head on her forehead. "I fuckin love you. When are you going to get it though that daft brain of yours?" he groaned. "I would crush any fool dumb enough to hurt you," he said through clenched teeth. He shoved her away as his eyes rolled back in pain. He ran his hands through his dark brown and ginger hair while he fought to keep from crying out.

"Don't touch me...just don't," he whispered as he positioned himself back against the headboard.

Cashmere stood, biting her bottom lip while she watched him.

"I know you saw that photo album," he remarked as he waved his hand.

Yeah, the one that disappeared from the room, her mind pointed out.

"I also saw the two of you talking in the great hall."

Pike narrowed his gaze. His eyes sparkled with emotion as they bore into her. Even all swollen and bruised, he looked handsome. To be honest, it just added to his sex appeal. The closely tapered beard didn't hurt it either. He had a dangerous side to him that caused her body to quake. To know that a man was willing to fight to protect her; that he was willing to send a message that she was his, and back it up with his own body was absolutely soul melting to her.

"Maureen is gay."

"Bullshit."

"That's the same thing her family said. If you don't believe me, you can ask her now," he offered in a low voice as he pulled the cover over his lower half.

Cashmere turned just in time to see the tall, tanned blond glide into the room. It seemed as if the light blue skinny jeans she had on was made just for her to display her perfect figure. She finished off her outfit with a pair of tan ankle boots, and a pink top; that anyone with eyes could see her perky nipples through on account that she wore no bra at all. The woman had a natural beauty that didn't require no more than the red lipstick she had on her thin lips. Her medium length bob swayed as she walked and kept in time with her bouncing breast. Cashmere stole a look at Pike. He could clearly see her doubts that this woman was actually gay.

"I can see I'm interrupting, so I won't stay long. Hi, I'm Maureen," she introduced herself.

Cashmere took her hand and shook it.

"I just wanted to come by to check on you," she explained, no longing giving Cashmere a second thought.

"So you caught the fight?" smirked Pike.

"Not all of it. Just the half of the second and all of the third," she answered in awe as she tapped him on his raised knee. "Thank you for not breaking my Dad's windpipe," she chuckled.

"Shit, is the old man alright?" inquired Pike.

"He'll make it, but not that knee. He's going to have to get surgery for sure."

"I'm not paying his fucking bills," growled Pike.

Maureen tossed back her head and laughed. Even her laughter and airy voice was attractive. "Did you see the fight?" she asked, acknowledging Cashmere at last. Her brown eyes examined Cashmere from head to toe.

"Yes."

"He was a beast, but now that he's put the word out, you don't have to worry about anyone getting out of line. Have you seen a lot of the place? From what I've heard, he keeps you locked up."

Pike went still. He knew what she was doing, and even though they were friends, and she might just be teasing him, he didn't like it at all. He tilted his head and continued to listen to her chat Cashmere up from under hooded lids.

"I can show you around and-"

"Think about what you're doing, Maureen?" he interjected in a low voice, cutting her off.

The brown eyed blonde turned her head and met his green eyes. The coldness she found there made the smile she had on her lips slip for a second.

"Or maybe not," she stated, clearing her throat. "I can see that you're in very capable hands," she teased while she continued to eye Cashmere.

"Yes, I am. Would you bring me some food up here, Peaches?" he asked Cashmere, using the name he reserved for when they were having sex. He saw her brown eyes glaze over with lust from the use of the term. Her eyes strayed to his dick, knowing he was completely nude under the sheets. Quickly, he slid down further to hide his stiffing cock.

On their way downstairs, Maureen kept up the chatter until Cashmere cut her off. Not being the one to beat around the bush with another woman, she got right to the point.

"Are you really gay?"

The woman stumbled on the step before she turned around to glance back at Cashmere.

"I think the fact that I have this tattoo means I'm very committed to pussy," she chuckled.

She held up the underside of her wrist to show the ink she had there. It was an image of a very sexy kitty with her leg up, licking herself. Instead, of its fur being a typical color, it had been shaded in the rainbow colors of the LGBT community.

Cashmere's perfectly arched eyebrow went up. "It looks really nice, but you weren't always gay, so are you bi?" she questioned.

"If you're asking if I fucked Pike, the answer is yes. I fucked him, a lot, when we were younger," she sighed, leaning on the stone wall. "I know I should say that I was disgusted by it, but he was really good," she remarked as her eyes traveled down Cashmere's body, openly.

"You need to help me understand," hissed Cashmere as she waved her hand to tell the woman to get on with the story.

"It was good, but *not* great."

"Then there has to be something wrong with your coochie because Pike is an *amazing* lover."

"I'm sure he is because there *is* something wrong with my coochie. It likes pussy...not his dick or any dick as a matter of fact. I still accepted his proposal knowing that, though, cuz my family wanted to marry into money. Then our relationship became more of a friendship than anything. So, I told him the truth and broke it off," she explained.

"Then why the damn fight?" barked Cashmere.

"Because my dumb arse family can't understand that he had nothing to do with me being this way. They think that he *made* me gay. Don't ask me why," groaned Maureen, holding up her hand to keep Cashmere quiet. "They started that shit up as soon as they knew he was coming back. First with Demont. Then they stole a few sheep and cows. They busted up Angus' car, but Pike just ignored them. It took them fuckin with you to get the arse beating they deserved."

Maureen could see the magnitude of her words register in Cashmere's eyes. She switched the topic as she began walking down the stairs again. Back in the great hall, she turned to Cashmere. She reached into her *Michael Kors* hobo bag and pulled out a black bag.

"You left this at the store," she smiled. Leaning over, she kissed Cashmere's cheek while she placed the package in her hands. "Good luck," she whispered.

Chapter Eight

Cashmere froze as soon as she opened the room door. The sight of Pike trying to remain upright by holding onto the back of one of the leather chairs startled her. She kicked the door closed. Walking over to him, she laid the plate and glass of beer; she had in her hands on the small round table that sat between the two chairs.

"What are you doing?"

Pike glanced at her sheepishly. "Going to see if Marueen had her hand shoved down your pants."

She gave him a blank stare.

"You think it's a joke. I've seen her turn many straight girls out."

"Maybe she picked up some pointers from fuckin you back in the day," she sneered.

He shuffled around the chairs and took a seat with her sitting next to him in the other chair.

"You never told me why you went to town," he remarked, choosing to overlook her comment.

"I just wanted to get out for a while."

She could see him staring at her from the corner of her eyes. She wondered if his cousins told him the real reason why she wanted to go?

"I'm just happy you didn't go alone. If those fuckers would had-"

"You need to stop getting mad. Didn't you know that you turn full blown Irish when you do?" she smirked.

He laughed.

"I like it. It's actually very sexy," she admitted, licking her lips.

"In that case, lass, if it will keep your bock dripping wet and keep you in the mood for a scuttle, then I'll be talkin like this forever," he teased in his accent.

"What the fuck?"

"I said if it will keep your pussy wet and you in the mood to fuck."

His voice had deepened as he interpreted his words. The mood in the room changed instantly. Her body felt as if the large fireplace in front of them had been lit.

"No!"

Pike stiffened.

"You can look like that all you want. Nothing for the next few days."

"Come on, Peaches," he begged as he reached over the table to grab her hand in an attempt to pull her over. "I just had a close call. I need some," he whined.

She laughed at his pout. "You *won* the fight."

"I'll be happy to let you do all the work." He shifted his approach, watching her reaction. "We have a baby to create, and according to you, time is short."

He took note of the way she broke eye contact with him.

"I'm sure a few days will be ok," she stumbled.

Pike fought hard to keep his reaction from showing. His cousins had told him why she had gone to town.

***

Pike noticed the change in her after that day. He had tried to break her out of it, but her mood still remained closed off, three days later, and his patience with her was starting to run thin. He knew that it was going to be only a matter of time before she brought up going back home since the four weeks was just about at an end. He played over in his mind how he would respond which ranged from anger to threats; to just saying fuck it, and sending her on her way. Even still, he was determined for her *not* to keep his child, if she was that stubborn enough to go back to her lifestyle.

If she would just trust me, he thought, but he wasn't going to force her any more than he had already done.

"Where the hell is she?" he hissed, looking at the time on his cellphone. Last night she had disappeared too, he recalled.

Although the bruising was still there, it had only taken three days for the swelling to go down and for him to get back on his feet. Frustrated, he ran down the stairs, and down the halls. He peeked into the rooms as he went along only to come up short. She wasn't in any of them. He marched across the landing and headed toward the kitchen. He really didn't want to search the entire seventy thousand square foot home for her. He might be doing better, but too much walking wreaked havoc on his ribs.

"Have you seen Cashmere?" he sighed.

Demont closed the fridge door. "Ye, she been going to the lake at night," he responded with a shrug.

Pike stared into the distance for a second before he turned and left the kitchen. He didn't even worry about the fact that he was shoeless, or that the Irish night was chilly, and he was only in a tank top and gray low hanging basketball shorts. As fast as he could muster, he went to the stables, and hopped on a mount, bareback. He scanned the shoreline while the horse walked slowly as it had been commanded to do. Even in the dark, he didn't have a problem making out her form. She was standing calf deep in the midnight blue waters. The white color of her sundress reflected the light of the full moon. Quietly, he slipped from the horse and pulled on its reigns to ensure it didn't return to the stables.

"There isn't a *Lady in the Lake* in this one."

Cashmere jumped at the sound of his voice. "No, there's fairies."

He could hear the rawness in her voice which caused him to wonder if she had been crying. His heart contracted when he saw the tears that left streaks on her cheeks. He held out his hand.

"You don't have a coat. Come on."

Cashmere flashed him a crooked smile before she began to tread the water slowly towards him. He guided her to the side of the horse. He closed his eyes when he touched her leg to help her onto the animal. She had stayed true to her demand of no sex. He swung himself on the horse. Instead of heading back, he started down the shoreline of the lake.

"I'm sorry," he whispered against her ear. "I didn't know bringing you here would have made you so unhappy or the thought of having my baby. Whenever I want something, I just make a plan, and I get it...but I see that the heart doesn't work that way."

She dropped her head and sighed. "That's not what I was out here doing? Oh, I was praying. I've prayed to the God, the fairies, to every fuckin blade of grass, but *not* because I'm unhappy."

"Then why have you been so-"

"Because I don't know what to do," she cried. "I just want to know what to do."

Pike stopped the horse, grabbed her, and turned her around to face him.

"What do *you* want? Be honest with me. None of that tongue and cheek shit," he barked as he gazed down at her.

"You know what I want."

"No, I don't. I've been very clear while you're been silent. So, tell me...now."

"I want you. I've always wanted you...even when we were just friends, I wanted you, Pike," she admitted while she reached her hand up to touch his face.

He grabbed her hand and pulled it away, which surprised her.

"Then what's the issue?"

"What would your family say Pike or your friends? It's alright to fuck the bitch but never marry them."

He glared at her for her choice of words. "I've never seen you as my bitch."

"But others will because that's what I am. I'm a pro-"

The sound of Pike's hand connecting with the side of her face echoed throughout the night. He tightened his grip on the horse's reigns to keep it still.

"You fuckin hit me!"

"And I'll do it again if you don't start thinking for yourself. Every decision I've made since the age of seventeen was to ensure that I would be a man that made his *own* decision. I can take care of my damn self, so why the hell should I lose sleep over what my parents or anybody has to say about *my* life?"

"Goody for you, Pike...but everybody can't do that. I can't do that. I-"

"Why?" he pressed, searching her face.

"Look, you say you're happy now, but later on when you've gotten over your fascination, and you see that what you thought you had isn't enough-"

"I'm not a schoolboy, Cashmere. This isn't a crush."

"-Or I embarrass you, you'll-"

"Are you going to be giving lessons on how to suck dick?"

"No, why would I-"

"Then why would I be embarrassed? Tell me, Peaches."

She stiffened. There was something in his tone that made her stop. There was a softness in his green eyes all of the sudden.

"He told you?" she asked in a high pitched voice.

"No, I overheard you two talking."

"Oh," she said, lowering her head.

"Don't you ever drop your head like you're some beaten dog," he fumed, as he lifted her head with his finger under her chin. "Look at me," he commanded. He lowered his head to meet hers. "I wouldn't care if you couldn't spell your own name, I would still love you," he said with some much force and feeling that it made her sway. "I *will* teach you so when our baby is born; you can read to it every night."

She hadn't realized she had been holding her breath until she released it in a rush.

"I fuckin love you, Pike."

He threw back his head and sighed. "I'm so happy you finally said it because I didn't know what I was going to do if you tried to leave me," He confessed with a smile.

"I love you," she began to repeat like a crazy woman until he stole her words in his kiss.

It didn't take long for their kiss to turn into passion. His hands went under her dress. She tossed back her head moaning when his hand entered her panties to stroke her pussy before sliding his fingers into her moist, hot center. He jerked down the front of her dress to suckle hard on her nipples.

"I know we don't have to rush in the baby making now, but I need you, Peaches," he groaned against her breast. From the way she was wetting and riding his fingers, he was sure she needed it, too.

"You're right," she replied. Pushing his hand away and pulled down on the front of his basketball shorts to free his cock. He held her steady while she positioned herself on his lap, moved her panties to the side, and began to impale herself on his large dick. She rested her head on the crook of his neck. She took her time, wanting to enjoy the feel of his cock stretching her flesh inch after glorious inch. Pike took a firm hold of her hips, raised her up, then dropped her down hard; burying himself completely in her. His hands moved to her shoulders. He forced her down while he grinded his hips, forcing his cock deeper still.

"Shit," he grunted through clenched teeth.

"You're right," she replied, finding her voice at last. "There's no rush because I'm already pregnant."

Pike pushed her back to look into her eyes. He ran his finger over her lips. Cashmere smiled. She opened her mouth and stuck out her tongue. Pike narrowed his eyes. He remembered the first time they had been on this horse. He had commanded her to open her mouth and give him her tongue. However, this time… she was giving herself freely to him.

He clicked his teeth to signal for the horse to begin walking. He opened his mouth for her to have her way. With each step, their bodies rocked back and forth, making their lovemaking easy as the Moon beamed down upon them and the night fairies danced around them.

Epilogue

Eight months later, Cashmere waddled around in their room putting clothes away in the room. Whenever she thought back to the day he had brought her to his house in Long Island, she seemed to tear up. Of course, she didn't know if it was the hormones of being pregnant or the fact that he had the entire master suite and the nursery; he had built adjoined to their room, just as she had described it on that day in Ireland. Out of breath, she sat on the edge of the bed. She hated the fact that her hands had swollen to the point that she couldn't wear her wedding ring. She bit her lip as yet another wave of Braxton Hicks overtook her. Just as the nurse had told her after their fourth false alarm, she remained calm and breathed through it. She was so happy that her Aunt Fran had started to come by more often, since she hadn't spoken to her Mother, since telling her she wasn't coming back to the brothel. Even though her Mother was happy for her decision, she still didn't want to talk to her.

Downstairs, Pike opened the door before the visitor could ring the doorbell.

"Hello, Isobel," he greeted the nervous woman as he moved to the side to let her in.

"Thank you."

Isobel scanned the entry way of the large mansion. "Where is Cashmere?"

"Upstairs," he answered while he closed the door. "She doesn't know I asked you here."

"I didn't think so. I had found it strange that she would after being dead silence for so long."

Pike ran his hands through his hair. He motioned with his hand for her to follow him. He led her into a sitting room.

"I called you after talking to your sister, Duchess, and Angie."

"Ah, so you did some research," she frowned as she took a seat.

"You can say that. I wanted to know why you would cripple Cashmere the way you did? I couldn't understand why you would *want* her to live like that."

Isobel wished he would sit down. The way he was staring at her was making her nervous. He was dressed in all black as if he was going to a funeral.

"I thought I knew what I wanted, and I reflected what I wanted, at that time, on her without even realizing it. I was just like her. I wanted to please my mother, and I did exactly what she said, even if Cashmere or I got hurt from it," she tried to explain.

"That's what Fran said. She told me some wild stories about your Mom. It sounded like you could have had a much happier ending if you would have fought to have your own mind."

"That's true...I've missed a chance or two," she admitted as she dropped her head.

Pike stiffed upon seeing the same mannerism in her that he had seen in Cashmere. However, not as much, now that she had a self-confidence that was all her own and nothing that was given to her by him or no one else.

"I wanted to return the favor. If you hadn't helped me by sending Fran and Levi, I would have been hard pressed in stealing Cashmere away. I was hoping that you would stay for the baby. So that give you a few weeks to work your shit out with her."

Fran had already told him that Isobel had left the brothel.

She blinked back her tears. "Thank you," she cried. Wringing her hands, "What are you having?"

"I'll let her tell you," he remarked, then he paused. "Fuck it! It's a boy, but don't tell her I told you," he warned.

Isobel laughed. He realized that she had passed that on to Cashmere as well. If the woman was just like his wife, he knew he was going to love her.

"Come on," he smiled.

Isobel had him stop a few times along the way out of fear. Finally, he took her hand and led her onward. The woman was visibly shaking by the time they had reached the closed door.

"Deep breath," he whispered. Isobel was so pale; he didn't want her to pass out.

Not giving her the chance to turn and run, he opened the door.

Cashmere had been standing in the middle of the room trying to breathe through the pain. Instantly, her eyes widened at the sight of her mother standing in the doorway next to Pike. She worked her mouth to say something, but no words couldn't express what she was feeling at that second. Then finally, she found her voice.

"Mama," she said in a cracking voice.

"I know you don't want to see me but...I, I'm so very sorry," sobbed Isobel, still standing next to Pike.

He pushed her into the room, causing the woman to stumble forward.

"I just knew you were mad at me because I didn't come back and-"

"*Mad*! After you called me, I told all those bitches what I really thought of them and left. I'm so happy that my little Princess has her *Disney* ending."

Pike rolled his eyes and walked away. He had seen more than enough. Neither one of them was killing each other. Besides, he had his brother, Brick; he needed to beat some sense into before it was too late. Shit, why should he be the only one to be given a happy ending.

THE END!

Thank You so much for reading. Please, remember to leave a review on Amazon and Goodread.

I would really love to hear from U!

You can contact me FACEBOOK on my Sapphire Rose page

Or

On INSTAGRAM under CHRISTINESAPPHIREGRAY.

Keep reading to get a SNEAK PEEK of Brick's story which will be out later in May!

EXCERPT
COMING IN MAY

From the force that Pike pulled out the chair to sit down, he knew his brother was doing everything he could to keep his anger in check. Brick's eyes went to his brother's shaking leg. They both had the same tell. Whenever they were pissed and on the verge of opening the flood gates of their anger, they would start with the leg. Brick leaned toward his brother and open his mouth to speak.

Pike put up a hand to warn him to keep silent. Slowly, Brick clamped his mouth shut. He didn't know what had happened in Cashmere's room, but he wanted to fuck the sweet thing that was waiting for him upstairs before they left the brothel. He stole one more glance at Pike before he folded on his bet. He had taken enough of the two men's money that were also sitting at the table.

"Here," he offered Pike. "You keep playing for me while I go upstairs. Diamond should be ready for me by now. Will you be ready to go in an hour?"

"Yeah. You'll find me right here."

"You aren't going to; you know?" Whispered Brick.

His eyes widened slightly when Pike shook his head, no. With a shrug, he walked off to go seek his pleasure in the bed of one of the girls he usually chose. There was no need for him to state the obvious. His brother was in love with a woman that he could never have. He had nothing against Cashmere. He liked her, and if she wasn't in the world of ass, tits, cocks, and pussy, she would make a great addition to the family. However, she was the ring leader of a whore house. There was no damn way that it was going to work out between the two of them, no matter how much Pike willed it.

He shook his head as he strolled from the casino. He glanced at the group of women that attempted to wave him over to them. They were in the most exclusive brothel in the World. Once again, he couldn't believe the fact that Pike only paid to have his cock to be sucked due to the fact that he was pining over Cashmere. Brick looked forward to their twice a month visits to Ginger Island. It was the only time he allowed himself the pleasure of being with a woman. After he was tricked by a past lover, he didn't trust the many women that tried to bed him. The weeks between their visit he had o result to masturbating or when he was really hard up, he would stop by the one woman that he knew had no desire to have children because she was too damn vain to have one. Shit, he would slap the taste out of his own mouth if he came here and didn't get to stick his dick in at least two holes, three if the girl was willing.

***

Lakyta downed the double shot of tequila for the third time. She could almost hear Dustin's eyebrow raise as she poured another glass.

"Don't you think you've had enough for false courage," he asked, sarcastically.

"Maybe."

He was poised and ready to grab the bottle when she went in for another refill. He didn't want her to be using the little stunt she had cooked up as an excuse to drink. His friend of ten years had come a long way. He would be damned if he was going to let the stress that her father was putting her through to cover his own ass to driver her to drink again.

"Listen, we've been over this a million times. Nothing will go wrong. All you have to do is relax and go through the motions. When this is all done, you won't have to worry about anything," he promised her.

"You say that like you're so damn sure. It only gets me out of this bind, but what about the next one, because...there will be a next one."

"Then you'll come up with another brilliant idea."

Dustin leaned against the wall as he gazed at Lakyta. Her dark shin was absolutely stunning to him. He had never seen any woman with such smooth skin. He always liked it when it shined from the shea butter she would put on it. It was like she had been created for a block of priceless ebony. The fact that she gifted with piercing blue eyes due to the genetic phenomenon from her Somalin ancestry only added to her breathtaking features. His stared openly while she let the robe she had been wearing slip from her shoulders to fall from to the ground. Even though she wasn't an employee of the brothel, her outfit she was wearing truly fit the bill. The yellow colored satin camisole clung nicely to her full breasts. The matching thong and garter belt and black stockings made his mouth go dry. Her toned legs, round ass, and taunt stomach made his dick stiffen.

"Shouldn't he be here by now," she sighed, causing him to refocus on the task at hand.

"As a matter of a fact, yes," he answered as he moved toward the door. "I'm going to go. Don't worry. Everyone is in place, and they all know what to do. Now, you need to relax and let him do his job."

"Hum, his job...I might actually enjoy this after all," she chuckled at the stare he shot her. "Hell, I have to make it convincing," she smirked as she waved him out of the room.

Quickly, she ran over to the bar and downed two more shots before she switched out the lights and slipped under the sheets to wait for her savior to arrive. Thankfully, she didn't have to wait long.

Brick closed the door. He remained still for a moment to allow for his green eyes to adjust to the darkness. He smirked at the form that was laying in the middle of the bed. He kicked off his shoes, and began to pull off his coat as he walked over.

"No, don't turn on the lights."

"Whatever you want," he shrugged. She was obviously going for sexy and mystery this go around. He wasn't surprised. Diamond was always doing something different. She would wear different wigs, outfits, and even change her voice as if she was an actress to make their encounters different each time. He would be lying if he said he didn't appreciate the effort she put into her craft, but at the same time, he saw it as a waste of energy. As long as her pussy was right and he came, he could give two shits about all the foreplay.

"There isn't a lot of time. I hope you don't mind."

"You read my mind. I'm ready to get started," she agreed.

"Eagar, are we?" He chuckled.

"You have no fuckin idea."

"Well, let me give you what you need."

Lakyta stiffened at the feel of his callous hand when it slipped under her shirt. She opened her mouth to ask him what he was playing at, but his mouth was already on hers. Once again, she was shocked, but this time it was for a different reason.

His mouth feels good...like really fuckin good," the voice in her head pointed out.

Suddenly, she breathed in and was assaulted by his manly scent. She wished she would have at least cracked the curtain in the room to let the moon's light in to see how this man actually looked. She heard her own sharp intake of breath from the sensations he was creating in her body. His rolled her hard nipple between his fingers before he squeezed it hard. She was sure that it wasn't just the liquor that was making her heart race or was the cause of the slipperiness that was starting in her pussy. She allowed her body to melt as he laid her back onto the mattress.

Brick pushed her shirt up roughly. A deep moan escaped from the back of his throat as he opened his mouth wide to draw her nipple into his mouth. The way her body trembled under him registered in his mind. Diamond's performances in the past was never this good. He had to commend her later on such a genuine act she was giving him. Even her whimper sounded like an angel to the devil that was ready to fuck her till she was out cold. Her entire body felt new and strange at the same time, if that was even possible, he realized. Her skin felt softer. Her curves were much more pronounced, and her smell was a mixture of sweetness, and some flora that he couldn't place.

"Mum, you shaved for me," he whispered as he shoved his hand into her panties to cup her pussy. The last time he had been there he had told her that she need to trim her growing bush back. He was happy that she had taken his words to heart.

"That's it. Open those pretty thighs for me."

Of course, Lakyta knew that he was here to solve the problem that she was in. However, never in her wildest dreams did she think he would take things this far. At any second, she knew that all the fun that she was having at this point would be over. He would go his way happily with the fruits of his labor. While she went back to her own world to continue to live her life on her own terms for a little while longer.

Shit, it's just sex, she reminded herself. *No, correction. Just foreplay. Just enough to make my current problem go away.*

She was sure that he wasn't dumb enough to take it that far, she ensured herself as while she guided his hand to her throbbing pussy.

Brick paused for a split second after his fingers penetrated her cunt.

What the hell? His mind screamed.

There was no denying that this pussy didn't feel in no way shape or form like Diamond's. Diamond was good, but her pussy wasn't *this* good. There was a tightness that was never there with Diamond's due to the constant use of it. There were even times that he had to switch to anal to achieve his orgasm. Unlike this one that was hot, tight, and was currently dripping its juices down his fingers like a damn waterfall. He bit down on his bottom lips and let his eyes roll back in his head while his other hand went to unzip his pants. His cock sprung free, and with a mind of its own, began to buck at the thought of being surrounded by the moist walls of her cunt.

Without warning, he shifted. In one fluid movement, Pike rolled over between her opened legs and thrusted into her hard. The spell of lust, of fun, and games were broken immediately.

"Fuck," he shouted.

"Oh, my God," she cried out. His dick felt as if it had just rendered her in two.

Brick fumbled for the lamp on the night table that he knew was next to the bed. At that second, the room door swung open. He turned just in time to see a group of men flood into the room. His expression went from surprise to rage as the bright flashes from their camera phones went off.

"Get up, you asshole," he heard the woman underneath him demand while she did her best to push him off.

Lakyta went deathly still when his hand went around her neck. She began to claw at the hand that held her in a Kung-Fu grip as she fought to breathe.

He's actually strangling me. He's going to kill me, she acknowledged as the fear of reality gripped her.

Brick flicked on the light at last. He froze. His green eyes widened as he gazed down into the scared blue eyes of the most beautiful black woman he had ever seen. A black woman that *was not* Diamond. The same black woman that he still had his thick, throbbing cock buried deep in her wet, ungodly tight pussy. The black beautiful woman, that isn't Diamond whose pussy he was buried balls deep in, and there were now photos to testify to that fact. All the other facts he could process. However, it was the last fact that was causing his hand to tightened even more around her neck. No, that wasn't entirely true. He had seen those eyes before, he recalled. He examined the gasping woman's face. There was no way that she wasn't the same girl, now a woman.

The plot thickens, he thought.

"What the hell are you doing here, Lakyta? What the hell have you just done?" he growled.

Looking for a publishing home?

Royalty Publishing House, Where the Royals reside, is accepting submissions for writers in the urban fiction genre. If you're interested, submit the first 3-4 chapters with your synopsis to submissions@royaltypublishinghouse.com.

Check out our website for more information: www.royaltypublishinghouse.com.

Be sure to LIKE our Royalty Publishing House page on Facebook

Made in the USA
Charleston, SC
09 August 2016